12/23/17

Also by Rae Foley
in Large Print:

The Velvet Web
The Shelton Conspiracy
No Hiding Place
Wild Night
Call it Accident
Fatal Lady
The Man in the Shadow
Dark Intent
Nightmare House
Sleep Without Morning
Dangerous to Me
Death and Mr. Potter
It's Murder, Mr. Potter
Girl from Nowhere

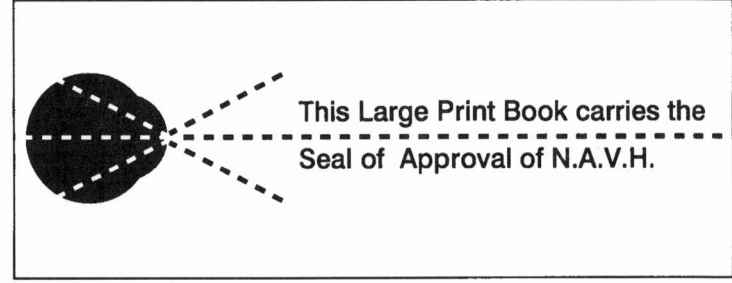

This Large Print Book carries the
Seal of Approval of N.A.V.H.

FEAR OF A STRANGER

RAE FOLEY

G.K. Hall & Co.
Thorndike, Maine

Published in 1997 by arrangement with Golden West Literary Agency.

G.K. Hall Large Print Romance Collection.

The text of this Large Print edition is unabridged.
Other aspects of the book may vary from the original edition.

Set in 16 pt. Plantin by Minnie B. Raven.

Printed in the United States on permanent paper.

Library of Congress Cataloging in Publication Data

Foley, Rae, 1900–
    Fear of a stranger / Rae Foley.
       p.   cm.
    ISBN 0-7838-8327-7 (lg. print : hc : alk. paper)
    1. Large type books.   I. Title.
[PS3511.O186F4   1997]
813′.54—dc21   97-40239

FEAR OF A STRANGER

CHAPTER 1

The letter came just as Kay was beginning to listen for Ernest's knock. The speed with which she ran to answer the door was, she admitted to herself, a dead giveaway, so she was relieved to see only the somewhat surprised face of the elevator man.

"This just came, Miss Forbes."

"Thank you." Her tone was detached, but she was aware that he would unerringly associate her eagerness with the arrival of Ernest, and she felt herself flushing.

The letter marked "special delivery," was in Uncle Paul's crabbed writing. Every year it grew smaller, more pinched. Like Uncle Paul himself.

Standing in the middle of the room, she ripped open the envelope and then moved closer to the huge window with its breathtaking view of lower Manhattan to make out that difficult script, the words run together as though, she thought with a pang of pity, Uncle Paul were unwilling to waste even space.

The change in him had been so gradual that she had been almost unaware of it until the harm had been done. Curious that brothers with the same heritage, the same upbringing, the same environment, could be so unlike. Her father, the younger of the two, had been big and jovial and openhanded. He had also, Kay was aware, managed to run through most of his money until Paul had insisted on taking over its management. But at least her father had loved living, had warmed both hands before the fire of life. Uncle Paul's hands were chilly. He had approached all experience with caution and distrust. Unmarried, he had remained at the farmhouse in Connecticut, which, on her annual duty visits, she had found bleaker, more cheerless, more dilapidated. Even his food had become increasingly spartan, and his clothes were threadbare.

"Let your father throw away his money," Paul remarked tartly in response to her protests. "When it is gone, he will be singing a different tune. I've got to think of my old age."

All these years Paul Forbes had been thinking of his old age. Her father had held the days lovingly in his hands and had enjoyed them to the top of his bent, but he had died at sixty and his younger brother still lived at sixty-five. Paul had been right in a way, Kay acknowledged, though it was not her way; even now when the last of her money was running out; even now when the future was a complete blank, a leap into the unknown.

A year earlier the future had stretched ahead as clearly charted as a road map. That was when she had been making her preparations to marry John. Then, a week before the date set for the wedding, John had died in a multiple car crash during a fog on the Garden State Parkway from which she herself had escaped with a mild concussion. Unfortunately, an overeager reporter at the time had used the words "brain injury," a phrase that people were inclined to remember and speculate about when the accident left her with raging headaches that recurred for months.

A needless, senseless tragedy that had drained the light from the sky and left her adrift, motiveless. Little by little, she had picked up the pieces. She was not, she told herself fiercely, going to live in the past as Uncle Paul postponed living for his old age. She was going to begin again, find a new road, a road that might even, in time, be sunlit, not misted over with the fog in which John had died.

Against the dark of a late winter afternoon lights began to appear in tall office buildings, working their nightly miracle. Kay drew a breath of sheer delight. If she had to give up her apartment on lower Fifth Avenue, she would miss all that, but there was bound to be something else, something interesting, something unexpected.

She remembered the letter in her hand, deciphered it slowly, frowning. It was curiously disturbing. He had, Uncle Paul wrote, suffered a heart attack. His bewilderment and a kind of outrage that this could happen to a man of exemplary behavior were clear to read. The foundations on which he had put his trust had given way. He had obeyed all the "thou shall nots." He had let all his todays slip by so that he might

9

be safe and secure tomorrow, and now it appeared that there might be no tomorrow.

According to his doctor — and what they charge for a house visit! — the heart muscle was gravely impaired There might, probably would, be other attacks. The greedy quack had done little except to prescribe drugs and to warn him to live quietly, without worry or excitement. The old fool!

"I want you to come at once, Kay. In the long run it will be worth your while. After all, you are the only family I have. And I want you to stay here. I need someone to protect me."

Kay held the letter closer to the light. Yes, the word really was *protect.*

"You are not the nervous sort of woman, thank god! Not afraid of your own shadow. Come as soon as you can. Your loving Uncle Paul."

He was afraid to die. The letter was brimming over with fear, and he expected her to hold death at bay for him.

Kay picked up the telephone. However urgent his need might be, Paul had not called her because a long distance telephone call would cost more than a special delivery stamp.

"I'll come up tomorrow," she promised.

"You'll plan to stay awhile, won't you, Kay? You won't want to rush back to New York at once?"

Responding to the appeal in his voice, she promised rashly, "I'll stay as long as you want me."

Some of the exhilaration with which she had looked forward to the evening faded. She wondered bleakly how long Ernest Billings would remain interested in a girl who was out of reach. There would always be women eager to relieve his loneliness; that is, if he should be lonely without her. She might have been taking too much for granted.

There was a knock at the door and she went, this time sedately, without revealing haste, to admit him. An eddy of fresh air seemed to come in with him. Part of Ernest's charm was the illusion he gave of bringing fresh air into a room. Something in his sheer animal vitality charged the atmosphere around him. Though he was not above average height, he appeared to take up a great deal of space because of his wide, sweeping gestures. His superb health was emphasized by the assiduous use of a sunlamp. "More painless than a trip to Florida," he explained.

He pulled off his overcoat and stood smiling at her. "Hello, my lovely. You should always wear red. Its wonderful with your dark hair."

"I like men who notice a woman's clothes."

"I like women with clothes worth noticing."

"My friend Charlie Hammond tells me I'm always right about clothes and wrong about people." Kay laughed as she spoke, but the comment still rankled. Charlie, she remembered, had never really liked John though he had tried hard for her sake.

"Charlie Hammond? Guy who married the Forrest money?"

"He married Sylvia Forrest." Kay's tone was rather curt. As Ernest made a half-laughing gesture of apology, she said, "They have a place near Uncle Paul's farm in Connecticut and they are about the nicest people I know. Charlie really is talented, a musician, working hard composing a light opera."

"Why do that when he doesn't need to work?"

"But he wants to. Wasn't it Bacon who said that idleness is the holiday of fools? Charlie loves his work."

"The industrious apprentice." There was laughter in his voice. "How strongly you believe in the importance of being earnest."

Kay started to retort and checked herself with an effort. John had once warned her, half amused, half annoyed, about a disconcerting habit she had of implying criticism of people. "Nothing one can fight," he had said, "because you don't come right out with it, but you make people feel that they fall short in some way. You set up impossible standards." His reproof had dissolved. "This austerity doesn't fit with your personality; it doesn't fit with the promise of your mouth," which he had covered with his own to illustrate his meaning.

Before leaving the apartment, Kay stopped for a moment, as she always did, for a last look at the lights that had transformed lower Manhattan into a wonderland. Standing beside her, his hands resting on her shoulders, smiling at her rapt expression, Ernest exclaimed, "How you love life!"

"Don't you?" she asked in surprise.

He thought about her question. "I like challenges, I enjoy excitement, but that's not quite the same thing, is it?" He laughed and his hands tightened on her shoulders. "Let's go out and enjoy some."

And they did. "I don't remember," Kay remarked while they were dancing after dinner and a theater, "ever having laughed so much in my life."

"It agrees with you. It's very becoming."

Back at their table they found fresh drinks waiting for them. "But I don't really want another," Kay protested.

"It will be good for you." He lifted his glass. "To us, Kay." For once his tone was serious.

Her eyes leaped to his, a question in them. He set down his glass and she noticed what well-shaped hands he had. By any standard he was a good-looking man, his appearance enhanced by his infectious gaiety. Now, however, he was sober.

"I want you to marry me. I'm mad about you, Kay. That won't be news to you. Will you take the matter under advisement, or whatever the proper phrase is?"

To her own surprise she hesitated. "We don't really know each other very well, do we?" she asked, troubled.

13

"I know I'm in love with you. Completely. Absolutely. Permanently. There's nothing else I need to know. Or want to know. How about you?" When she did not answer, he suggested "Do you require a brief account of my life, or references from unimpeachable sources? Health — good; disposition — excellent; ambition — well, at the moment that is centered on you, but I'll try to meet your standards. In a way, darling Kay, you are a calculated risk."

It was that word standards, an echo of John's complaint, which stilled the questions on her lips, though there were many things she wanted urgently to know. She knew nothing of his background, she had never heard him speak of his family, she had no idea what kind of job he held. An unknown quantity, though an engaging one.

"Declaration filed," Ernest said. "Please do not overlook."

"Declaration received and contents noted." Her tone promised more than her words. What in the world had made her hesitate?

He smiled at her, his face alight, and signaled for his check. "Let's get out of here."

While they waited for a cab, he asked, "May I come up for a few minutes?"

"Not tonight, Ernest. It's terribly late."

"But I haven't even kissed you yet. If you knew how long I have waited! Weeks and weeks."

She laughed. "There's a lot of time ahead."

"Tomorrow?"

"Tomorrow," she agreed. Then, in sudden

recollection, "Oh no, Ernest! I can't."

"Don't be absurd. Of course I'll see you to-morrow."

"I'm going to Connecticut in the morning and I may have to stay up there some time."

"But, Kay —"

"This is something I must do." She explained the situation.

"I am not being put aside for any uncle." He hailed a cab. "If it's too late for your apartment — doorman and all that — come to my place for a little while. We've got to talk. You can't simply go off in the blue."

"Well, just fifteen minutes, then."

"Fifteen minutes," he agreed. "I'll hold a stop watch."

His apartment was on the first floor of a re-modeled town house below Grand Central, with long windows, high ceilings, and a big fireplace. The beautifully proportioned living room had been furnished in unobtrusive good taste.

"How nice this is!" Kay exclaimed.

"It doesn't have your wonderful view, but I've tried to make it comfortable and, of course, the location is convenient. May I fix you a drink?"

"Heavens, not another, unless you have some orange juice."

"Can do. One orange juice coming up."

While he busied himself in the kitchenette, Kay wandered around the room, looking at the books, the records, the pictures, seeking, though she did not admit it to herself, some clue to the man she found so attractive and about whom she knew so little.

When Ernest returned with two glasses of orange juice, she pulled the letter from her evening bag.

"Read it for yourself and then you'll understand why I have to go."

"I don't get this," he admitted when he had finished the letter. "He sounds odd doesn't he?"

"He is frightened and not just by the idea that he is going to die. There is something else. Ernest, I've simply got to go."

He looked through the letter again. Watching him, substantial and assured, Kay felt her heart lift. Ernest would take care of things. She would never again have to face problems alone.

"He seems to be dangling bait to get you there, Kay. I don't much like the sound of that."

"You don't understand Uncle Paul. He distrusts everyone. He thinks people act only in their own interests."

"Well, so they do, basically; they just try to find other reasons that sound better, but, after all, man's chief drive is self-preservation."

"You don't really believe that, do you?"

"You're so — untouched, Kay. The world isn't all that good. People learn to look for the angles."

"People like Joe Simon?" When Ernest looked at her without comprehension, she said. "You can't have forgotten. The man who dragged all those people out of the burning tenement. He was just a passer-by and they were strangers to him, but he risked his life over and over and he was left horribly crippled and disfigured for life."

"I don't remember."

"But it happened not more than six months ago and the papers were full of it; there were big stories on radio and television. You can't have forgotten."

"Six months ago?" He frowned and then his face cleared. "That accounts for it. I was out of the country six months ago."

"You were? I didn't know that. Where did you go?"

"Well — say it was a mission, but please don't say it too loud." He held her eyes in a kind of voiceless message and then he returned to the letter. "So he is going to make it worth your while."

Aware that, having issued his warning, Ernest wanted the subject of his foreign trip dropped, Kay said, "Uncle Paul is just reminding me that I'll come into whatever he has to leave."

"Is it so much that he can afford to crack the whip?"

"I have no idea, but as he is a very astute man at investing money and he never spends an un-necessary penny, it is probably quite a lot. Though, of course I'm not going because he cracked the whip. I'm going because he is a sick man and he is frightened of something."

Ernest's warm hand clasped hers. "You don't need to tell me that, dear. I think I know you

17

better than you know yourself. And of course you must go. But I'm going with you, and there's to be no argument. There's a kind of feeling about that letter; I don't want you running into something unpleasant, something wrong."

Something wrong. That was what Kay herself had thought, but she had tried to dismiss the idea. Imagining things had been her weakness always. "Overimaginative," her report card had read when she was eight. "A tendency to dramatize situations," a teacher had remarked when she was in high school. She had found something shameful in these comments, but they had not seemed to curb her wayward imagination.

Ernest did not give her time to think of excuses. "I'll call for you at — how far is it?"

"Just about seventy-five miles."

"Will ten-thirty be all right? We'll have lunch on the way."

She felt a wave of relief but protested as a matter of form, "Won't that interfere with your job?"

"You are my job now." He looked at her, unsmiling. Then he tilted back her head and kissed her.

It was nearly two when Ernest left her in the lobby. It was after seven when she locked the last suitcase. All night she had gone back and forth from her bedroom, selecting and packing clothes that would be suitable for the country, to the living room where she paid bills and wrote notes breaking appointments and explaining her sudden departure.

There was no point in making any far-reaching plans. Everything depended on Uncle Paul's condition. Perhaps she could arrange to get a male companion for him. Perhaps he would have to go into a nursing home.

She wished that she and Ernest had had time in which to discuss the future. Would he want to maintain this apartment, which her father had bought for her several years earlier? Could he afford to maintain it? She didn't, Kay realized, have the faintest idea how much money he earned. She didn't even know what his job was. "You are my job now," he had told her.

She put down her pen, laughing aloud in the room. This was ridiculous. She had practically committed herself to Ernest, and she knew almost nothing about him, his background, his activities, his ambitions. She didn't know what family he had. She didn't know whether he had ever been married before.

They had had adjoining seats at a big theatrical party for charity and had fallen into conversation. From then on he had been her constant escort. In those three months she could not recall any time when they had talked seriously. They had laughed a lot. They had established an easy companionship until the past few weeks when Ernest's attitude had changed, when she had become aware that their relationship was different, that the hitherto easygoing man would not be content indefinitely with casual friendship, that she did not want him to be content with it.

Now the future was bright again though not, perhaps, very clear. An uncharted world. "Say it was a mission." Kay stared out of the window, only dimly aware of snow brushing against the pane. "But don't say it too loud." And he had changed the subject.

A mission. For the government? That would account for his curious reticence about the work he did. Perhaps when — if — she married him there would be other missions about which he would be equally silent. Times when he would leave her and she would have to wait out his absence, not knowing where he was, what he was doing, when he would return. Times when he might be in danger and no one would tell her.

There was a strange quality to the breaking day. Snow was beginning to fall heavily, blotting out the city, a white shroud like the fog in which John had died, the fog in which she had killed him.

CHAPTER 2

It was still snowing when Kay prepared to leave the apartment. Winter seemed unwilling to loosen its grip on the shivering city. She could not recall any previous year when snow had fallen so late in the season. The snow was already deep in the streets, falling like a white wall, when Ernest picked her up and shoved her suitcases into the back of the big Cadillac. The luxury of the car somewhat surprised Kay. Ernest must be doing very well indeed. He had had it about a week, he told her in answer to her question.

"Sorry to be late," he said. "One of those domestic crises. I lost a cuff link and I must have spent twenty minutes hunting high and low for the thing." He grinned at her. "I need a wife to handle these little chores for me."

"And set out your slippers by the fire, I suppose."

"Naturally."

On the West Side Highway he kept an even forty miles an hour, the wipers doing their valiant best to maintain some visibility.

"What a horrible day!" Kay exclaimed. "I can't even remember a snowstorm so late in the season. I feel ashamed, letting you in for this."

He laughed as he pulled the car out of a skid

and slowed to a cautious thirty. "Would you have preferred driving yourself?"

She shivered. "I'll never drive a car again. Never!"

"That doesn't sound like you. Somehow I see you as a girl who simply drinks up all kinds of experiences."

"I killed a man once," she said somberly.

The wheel jerked in his hands but he did not take his eyes off the treacherous road. He said, his big, resonant voice subdued for once, "What on earth are you talking about?"

"It was a year ago last summer. The man I was going to marry had driven me down to the Jersey shore. He had a new car that we planned to take out to the Coast on our honeymoon. He let me drive back and we rolled into a heavy fog. No warning. Just all of a sudden it was there, all around us. We piled up on the car ahead, a car behind crashed into us. John was killed. I got off with a slight concussion."

"Thank God for that, at any rate!" Ernest changed the subject abruptly. "Now tell me about this uncle of yours, not just because I don't want to make any blunders when I am introduced to your family but because that letter of his sounded queer."

"He's not senile, if that is what you are suggesting so tactfully. Except that he is growing rather eccentric in some ways, there is nothing wrong with Uncle Paul's mind."

With Ernest's prompting she told him about

the Forbes family. They had come to America during colonial days, moved from Massachusetts to Connecticut and had, unlike most restless Americans, retained their roots in New England though they had drifted out to Ohio. In time her grandfather had built a modest fortune in steel. Her father had let his share of the money slip through his fingers like sand. He was a man who liked to experience everything. By the time of his death his money would have disappeared altogether if Uncle Paul had not insisted on assuming its management. Paul himself had returned to the old farmhouse in Connecticut, which the family had built generations before, and settled there, hoarding his own share of the family fortune.

"Not literally, of course," Kay explained "but he has become more and more frugal. That letter was typical. He wanted urgently to have me come, but he wrote rather than pay for a long-distance telephone call. He lives like a hermit, seeing almost no one but the woman who comes in mornings to clean and cook for him and who has a difficult time of it, poor dear."

"What do you mean — a difficult time?"

Kay laughed. "Last time I was up there she complained that she couldn't be expected to cook a decent meal — and she's a superlative cook — when she wasn't given anything to cook with. I think by that time Uncle Paul had begun to dole out the supplies to prevent waste."

"A regular miser, then!"

"Oh, no. Well, yes, I suppose he is. You'll be horribly uncomfortable at the farmhouse, Ernest."

"That won't matter." He slowed to twenty miles. The snow was so heavy now that it was like driving through a white curtain. Now and then the dark bulk of a car loomed through the snow, but for the most part the highway north of New York was empty of traffic. Without the shelter of city streets they became aware of the increasing force of the wind, so strong that at times the heavy car shuddered under the impact.

"It's going to be a real blizzard!" Kay exclaimed in distress.

"Good. That will be a new experience for me. I grew up in the south and I missed big snowstorms and all the winter sports. Perhaps if your uncle is well enough for you to leave him now and then you can initiate me."

"What part of the south? You know it's really absurd how little I know about you."

"Georgia, but I haven't been back in years. No family left, so there's nothing to take me back. Anyway, it's not the past that counts, only the future. I want to talk about our future, Kay. When will you marry me?"

"We can't decide anything definite until we know what Uncle Paul's condition is. There may be unexpected difficulties. Anyhow, I simply can't abandon him if he is frightened. It would be too cruel."

"But as soon as possible. Say in a month?"

"Ernest, don't be ridiculous! Aside from Uncle Paul, there's a lot of planning for us to do."

"A white-satin wedding with ushers and bridesmaids?" He sounded resigned but not enthusiastic.

"No, I don't care about the trappings, but we would have to decide where we are going to live. Things like that."

"If you like it as much as you seem to, we couldn't do better than keep your apartment. It's charming."

"But rather expensive to maintain," she said tentatively.

He grinned. "Maybe miserliness is inherited."

"Well, I didn't know," she defended herself. "I just thought —"

"I'm thinking, too. If we don't have something to eat before long, I'll probably faint in your arms. I left home without breakfast."

She laughed. "I know a good inn that's open all year round if you can hold out for another thirty minutes."

He considered the matter. "I can manage, but only if we pull off the road while I kiss you properly."

The snow had begun to taper off by the time they had eaten a leisurely and excellent lunch. The highway had been cleared and sanded, but visibility was still poor and there were icy patches that required caution. When they left the main highway, driving conditions worsened. The side roads were less well cleared. After skidding sev-

25

eral times, Ernest slowed to a bare fifteen miles an hour.

"You take the next turn on the right," Kay said at length, "and it's a little stinker. A sharp turn, cross a narrow bridge over the ravine, and then a really steep climb up a hill. And we'll be lucky if it's been cleared at all."

Ernest cautiously maneuvered the car across a narrow, slippery bridge, whose railings were concealed by snow. Even in low gear the Cadillac labored, skidded, lost traction, and slid backward. The road had been plowed but not sanded, and it looked like a tunnel with snow piled high on either side.

"If you can make it up this rise, you'll be all right. The farmhouse is just over the top."

"A little sand wouldn't have hurt," Ernest grunted.

"I suppose they didn't bother because Uncle Paul and the Hammonds have the only houses up there; the Hammonds are spending the winter on the Riviera and Uncle Paul leaves the place so seldom that the road isn't much used."

"We'll make it." Ernest put the car into reverse, let it roll to the bottom of the incline; then with a roar it rushed at the hill, swerved sickeningly toward a snowbank, righted itself, and was once more on level ground.

For a moment they sat quiet in the car relaxing from the strain. Then Ernest lighted a cigarette and looked at the gracious white house.

"It's a beautiful place, Kay! I had no idea it

would be so impressive. Colonial architecture at its comely best, And I like that big red barn against the snow."

"It's not used as a barn any more. Years ago it was converted into a studio when my father took up painting for a while. In my opinion, it's much the most attractive part of the whole estate, but it hasn't been used for years."

"How much land is there?"

"About eighty acres. I'd like you to see the place properly. On a clear day there is a terrific view, one that almost justifies the steep hill you have to climb to get here." She shuddered. "There was one awful moment when you skidded on that little bridge and I thought we would both go into the ravine. I'm so glad you are here, Ernest. I'd have been terrified coming up the hill in a taxi, even if I could have found one to drive me from the station on a day like this."

He pulled her into his arms, his lips moving over her face. "I'm glad I'm here, too." As she released herself, smiling, he said, "I thought your uncle was alone. Someone seems to be here."

Kay looked around. "Oh, the dilapidated Ford belongs to Uncle Paul and the jeep is Mrs. Brundle's. She's the housekeeper and so fat I never understand how she manages to squeeze behind the wheel. There's no garage and Uncle Paul's car seems to be completely buried. Not that it matters; he probably hasn't driven in weeks and it is unlikely now that he will ever drive again."

As she opened the door, Ernest warned her,

"Be careful not to slip and get inside as quickly as you can. I'll take care of the luggage."

After the warmth of the car the icy air cut off Kay's breath. It must be below zero, she thought, as she pulled her fur hood tightly around her face. Underfoot the frozen snow squeaked as though protesting at this invasion.

As she approached the house, she noticed the scaling paint, the sagging porch, caught her foot and nearly sprawled over a broken step. Uncle Paul was definitely worse. Even six months ago he would never have let the house fall into this state of dilapidation. She tried the door, which was locked, and then banged on it.

"Who is it?"

"Kay. Let me in, for heaven's sake; I'm freezing." She waited impatiently for chains to be removed, bolts shot back, a key turned in the lock. Surely it had not been this bad on her last visit during the summer.

The woman who opened the door was short and immensely fat. She gave Kay just room enough to slide through and then slammed the door shut again.

"Wait," Kay said as the housekeeper was about to fasten a chain, "my fiancé drove me up. He's bringing the suitcases."

"Fiancé! Well, it's about time. Nearly twenty-seven aren't you?"

"One foot in the grave," Kay agreed cheerfully.

"I hope you know what you are doing. Any more trouble with your head?"

Nothing would ever convince Mrs. Brundle that Kay had not suffered permanent damage as a result of that "brain injury." Kay swallowed. I am not going to get angry the very first thing, she told herself firmly but without any real conviction. Inevitably she became enraged with Mrs. Brundle. The shaming factor in this was that Mrs. Brundle meant well. A widow with an invalid daughter, she had managed to maintain her small cottage in the village, to pay heavy fees to the doctor who was constantly being called upon to treat the endless maladies of poor Nelly, and to work herself into a lather to please such unreasonable employers as Paul Forbes.

Mrs. Brundle, as Kay frequently reminded herself, was a pathetic and gallant woman, but she did manage to say something unforgivable whenever she opened her mouth, and she talked endlessly. When she ran out of breath, which was often, she grasped the arm of her captive audience to frustrate escape, and wheezed until she could go on. Neither of these qualities deserved the exasperation they aroused in Kay. For a person as ridden by a sense of guilt as she knew herself to be, none of this self-knowledge was particularly helpful.

"Mr. Forbes expected you to come in time for dinner, and I made a big kettle of clam chowder. Unless you can have it for your supper, it's just going to waste. I didn't fix anything else; there's enough for a coupla days."

"We'll manage."

As usual the house smelled of beeswax and cleaning powders. The wide floor boards shone with polish. An old chest, which some seafaring ancestor had brought back from his travels, had been rubbed until it was like a mirror. The house was lovely, and certainly it was spotless, though the rugs were threadbare and the hallway much too cold for comfort.

The car door slammed and snow crunched under Ernest's firm tread. Kay flung open the door of the living room on the left and shrank back as she felt the chill.

"There's no heat in here!"

"Your uncle don't use that room and he says there's no sense in wasting good fuel oil. He sits in the other room when he can get downstairs."

Kay opened the outside door for Ernest, who was laden down with her suitcases, and one of his own.

"Where do you want these?"

"You can take them upstairs later. This is Mrs. Brundle, who looks after Uncle Paul. My fiancé, Mr. Billings."

Mrs. Brundle inspected him candidly. "Looks like he can take care of you." Her false teeth clicked as she turned to bolt the door, turn the key in the lock, and attach a heavy chain.

"This place is like a fortress! Kay was half amused, half appalled.

"No one gets in here. As I was telling poor Nelly just last night —"

From long experience Kay broke in smoothly

"You will yet," she assured him.

There was a faint twinkle in the tired eyes. "You're a liar but a nice one, Kay. Who is the man you brought up here with you?"

"His name is Ernest Billings and I am probably going to marry him."

"Trustworthy?"

She felt a spurt of anger, but she said calmly, "Of course he is trustworthy."

He grunted. "No of course about it. You always were a fool about people."

"I must be; I can even see some good in you."

He chuckled. "You've changed a lot since last summer. Kind of subdued then; banked down. I guess that was because you hurt your head. I was talking to Dr. Grantling about that not long ago; he wondered whether you still had your headaches."

"I had a mild concussion, as I have told you a hundred times. I did not suffer a permanent brain injury."

"Well, the fire is burning now, all right." Unexpectedly he added, "You always were kind of an alluring-looking woman." He yawned

"I'm sorry we disturbed your nap."

"I don't mind being disturbed. You're here and that's the main thing. Anyhow, I don't sleep much these days. Maybe it will be better with you around, you and your young man. Active sort, is he?"

"Active?" she repeated in surprise.

on the interminable saga of Nelly. "Has anyone tried?"

"Not that I've seen with my own eyes. But your uncle has noticed a man hanging around several times. And to my knowledge people don't loiter when it's below zero just for the fun of it." She opened the door of the living room on the right, which was unchanged except that it, too, had become shabbier; the soft colors in draperies and upholstery and rugs had faded until they were almost white. Kay looked at the thermostat, set at fifty-eight, and turned it up to seventy-two.

Mrs. Brundle winced. "Your Uncle won't like that."

Kay tried to be reasonable. "But the house is an ice box!"

"Well, staying in bed like he does most of the time — those stairs are a caution and it's a wonder to me he ain't broke his neck — he don't need so much heat. Anyhow, like I was saying to Nelly —"

"If you'll make up a bed for Mr. Billings —"

"The radiators are turned off in all the bedrooms except your uncle's and yours."

Kay's tenuous patience snapped. "Then turn them on, for heaven's sake!"

Mrs. Brundle heaved a sigh, clicked her teeth, and went out. They heard her climbing the stairs, moving slowly and so heavily that she shook the house and made the crystals of the chandelier send forth a clear, sweet note.

Laughing, Ernest put his arms around Kay.

"There's no place like home."

"I'm past apologizing for this house."

"I'll survive; we both will. I have a bottle of marvelous rum in my suitcase. If you can provide glasses, we'll try to warm up."

While Ernest wrestled with ice cubes, Kay looked around the kitchen. The big table was set for two, indicating that Uncle Paul was saving heat in the dining room, too. There were padlocks on the supply cupboards, bolts and chains on the back door and the door leading to the cellar, which had not been there during the summer.

Ernest poured rum, added water, and handed her a glass. "To our home away from home."

"This isn't funny," she said soberly. "Poor Uncle Paul. Either he is cracking up or —"

"Or he is really afraid."

"But what can he possibly be afraid of?"

Ernest shrugged. "God knows. Maybe just things that go bump in the night."

They carried their drinks back to the living room. The furnace had come on with a protesting thump as though it weren't accustomed to so much exertion. Warmed by the rum, they removed their coats. Voices from upstairs alerted them and Kay slid off Ernest's lap, straightening her hair. In a few minutes Mrs. Brundle came into the room.

"You woke your uncle outen his afternoon nap, so you might as well go talk to him. Only don't get him upset; the doctor don't want him worried."

"I won't worry him. Ernest, will you take the luggage? Mrs. Brundle, did you give Mr. Billings plenty of blankets? His room must like a refrigerator."

"I put that electric blanket you sent your uncle on the bed."

"Doesn't Uncle Paul use it himself?"

"He don't see the sense in wasting electricity when there's plenty of good blankets an quilts."

Kay shook her head helplessly. She had forgotten how steep and dark the stairs were. She guided herself with her hand on the railing This was no place for a man with a bad heart She would get Uncle Paul away from the house if she had to drag him, she vowed to herself She tapped on the door of the right-hand bedroom.

"Come in, Kay."

Paul Forbes seemed lost in the big double bed, a tuft of hair standing up on his head and making him resemble a Kewpie doll. A tiny man, not more than five foot three, he was like a mummy; his skin had a gray tone and his lips below the trim mustache were without color.

Kay bent over to kiss his cheek. "How are you, Uncle Paul?"

He snorted. "How do you think? I've had it. And damn it all," he added in an aggrieved tone, "I'm not ready to die yet. I was just getting to enjoy life. I figured if I were careful until I was sixty-five, I could afford to let myself go."

"I'd thought of getting a watchdog, but maybe he'll do just as well. Now if you'll get the hell out, I'll dress and come downstairs. I want to see this young man of yours for myself."

CHAPTER 3

While Kay unpacked a suitcase and changed to a wool sweater and skirt, she reflected with considerable satisfaction that Ernest had passed the first test with flying colors. You really couldn't know a person until you found out how he could meet emergencies and cope with discomfort. The hazardous drive he had welcomed as a challenge, seeming to enjoy it thoroughly. The cold discomfort of the house he had accepted cheerfully and with amusement. Nothing had daunted his high spirits.

She heard him in the hall speaking through the open door of Paul Forbes's room.

"Nice of you to let me stay, Mr. Forbes."

"I don't recall being given the choice," Paul commented, "but I don't suppose Kay would stay without you, and I need Kay."

"Let me help you with those shoes," Ernest suggested his good humor unimpaired. "Should you be up?"

"According to the congenital idiot who mispractices medicine in this community I should be dead," Paul retorted, "but as long as you are cluttering up the place, I thought I might as well get something out of you, have you help me up and down those confounded stairs." There was

36

no real animosity in his tone. "Hey, what do you think you are doing?"

"I'll carry you down. No, I can manage all right. Don't worry, I won't drop you."

Kay followed them down the stairs and into the living room, where Ernest deposited the sick man gently in a deep chair. A very sick man. He leaned back, eyes closed, struggling for breath. At length he broke in with irritation on Kay's worried comments.

"Leave me alone. Give me half an hour to rest and I'll be all right. Go away!"

They took him at his word, bundled up, and Kay, after getting the keys from Paul, who parted with them grudgingly, took Ernest out to see the converted studio. The big room had been oak-paneled, with a huge fireplace, carved oak chairs upholstered in red, and a window almost the length of the north wall. At one end a staircase led to a balcony off which there were two small bedrooms and a compact bath. Below there was a tiny but modern kitchen and a dark room whose door Kay had some difficulty in unlocking. She groped for the drop light in the middle revealing a storage area jammed with discarded furniture, rusty lawn mowers, and garden tools. She heard a rat scuttle across the floor and closed the door hastily.

"Good Lord," Ernest exclaimed, "your uncle must keep everything."

Kay laughed. "Believe it or not, there is even a cradle that belonged to my great-great-grandmother. I don't know whether we should try to clear the place out or just set fire to it, but something has to be done about the rats. Ugh!"

"The studio is perfectly charming," Ernest said. "Isn't it used at all? There must be countless artists who would give their eyeteeth to have a place like this in which to work. Sometimes I think space, freedom, and privacy are the only real luxuries. And here you have beauty as well. When we're married, let's keep this for a holiday house. Or would your uncle object?"

"I don't suppose he's been inside the place in ten years. He regarded art as a frivolity if not a minor vice."

As there were a series of explosions, Ernest asked, "What's going on?"

"Mrs. Brundle is leaving in her jeep." A blinding light made Kay blink and she turned toward the big window. The sun had come from behind a cloud and blazed on the huge icicles hanging from the eaves. Half closing her eyes against the glare, she went to peer out. The snow, blue-white, must be at least two feet deep, marked here and there by long deer tracks. Tree trunks held tufted patches of snow like cotton decorations against their trunks, and their branches were stark and bleak except for some hemlocks holding snow in their arms.

Some movement made her crane forward. A man on snowshoes was inspecting Ernest's car. With a quick look toward the window, which made her duck out of sight, he wrote down the license number. Again he looked toward the window and across the lawn to the house. He was quite young, with a long pointed upper lip that reminded her of portraits of Benjamin Franklin, his hair concealed by a wool cap.

As though unaccustomed to snowshoes, he moved away slowly and cumbersomely. There was something furtive about his behavior that disturbed Kay. Then he was on the incline and she watched him drop out of sight. She turned back from the window, frowning.

"Now what," she wondered aloud, "do you suppose he was up to?'

"Who?" Ernest asked. When she had told him, he said, "My license number? That's odd. Hey, do you suppose he could be the guy who frightened your uncle?"

"I don't know, but he acted furtive, and he didn't show up until Mrs. Brundle was out of the way."

"Suppose I have a talk with him and find out what he is doing here."

"He's gone."

"Well, he can't get far on snowshoes, and I have the car. If he is Mr. Forbes's loiterer, I'll put a stop to it, though I must say he'd have to be Houdini to break into that house."

"Be careful on the incline. The little bridge over the ravine is always slippery and the railing isn't more than a foot high. So far as I can tell, it is made of matchsticks."

She watched him go, smiling to herself. He represented strength and security and a kind of courage and confidence she lacked. When she returned to the house, Paul was sitting up in his chair, and both his color and his breathing had improved.

"Where's your young man?"

"There was someone on snowshoes snooping around. He wrote down Ernest's license number and Ernest naturally wanted to know why. He has gone after him to find out what the man is up to."

Paul stiffened. "Snooping around? What did he look like?"

"He was fairly young, I think. There was nothing special about him except that he had an unusually long upper lip that was pointed."

Paul lay back in his chair with a gasp.

"Ernest will be all right," Kay assured him. "He can cope."

"That young man of yours is an interfering fool. No need for him to talk to the fellow so long as he keeps him away from here. That's all I want."

"What's wrong?" Kay asked bluntly. "Is the man on snowshoes the one who has been frightening you?"

"Sounds like him."

"Who is he?"

"I don't know."

"But —"

"But I know what he is after."

"I did it for you," Paul said half an hour later. "I did it for the best."

She started to speak, bit back the words because he was so frail, so vulnerable. His life hung by a thread that could be snapped by a moment of anger or protest. But what on earth, she wondered helplessly, was she to do? He was terrifyingly exhausted by his long rambling confession, which had actually been a bewildered kind of self justification. And now he was in her hands.

She went over in her mind the jumbled, incredible story she had just heard. Not, of course, that she had heard it all. Perhaps Uncle Paul himself did not know it all, did not understand the basic insecurity that had driven him. Ironically, it was his fears that, in the long run, had betrayed him.

When her grandfather had died, dividing his fortune between his two sons, Kay's father set out to enjoy life. Paul, who had never had a gift for making friends, had already begun to withdraw, to distrust his fellowmen. Because he put no faith in the integrity of others and was convinced that everyone had an eye on his money, he determined to handle it himself, and he rejected all advice. To his stunned dismay he had lost everything through ill-judged investments while his brother, in spite of his extravagance, still had nearly half a million dollars.

It was then that Paul had urged his brother to let him handle his estate. His brother had refused impatiently until Paul had pointed out that this would be the best way to protect Kay's future.

"I made up my mind," Paul said earnestly, "that no one was going to touch a penny of that money. Not a penny. Anyhow, I don't see any good reason why the government should get its greedy hands on the savings my father accumulated through hard work. A bunch of crackpots who would just throw it away on a lot of nonsense."

"You mean you haven't been paying taxes?" Kay stared at him in dismay.

"Not a penny," he said triumphantly. "Taxes, in my opinion, are public theft."

"According to Oliver Wendell Holmes, taxes are the price we pay for civilization."

Uncle Paul snorted. What he had done, little by little, was to sell stocks and convert the money into currency — "It's all in hundred dollar bills, Kay" — which he had hidden in the farmhouse. No drop in the stock market could change its value. He hadn't spent an unnecessary cent on himself. She couldn't say he had. There it was, safe and sound.

Safe, that is, until two things happened. The first was the appearance of the man with the long upper lip. He had come around and asked unpleasant questions. Called himself a Treasury man, but Uncle Paul knew, after the first few minutes, that the fellow was a fake. Somehow he had gotten wind of the cache in the house. After that the place had been transformed, as far as possible, into an impregnable fortress.

The second incident was the heart attack followed by the grim warning from his physician that he had better set his affairs in order. So he had summoned Kay, not only to explain what he had done with her father's money, but to have someone young and active in the house to help him keep out intruders.

"You see," he looked at her rather doubtfully, "it's all for you. When I go, you won't have any inheritance tax to pay. No one knows the money exists."

"Except the man who has been hanging around," Kay reminded him.

"He can't get in. I've seen to that."

"But where is it, Uncle Paul?"

He felt in his pocket for a huge key ring, selected one of the keys. "This opens the padlock on that sea chest in the hall. Hurry. Your young man will be coming back."

Something in his desperate urgency silenced her protest. In the hall she bent over to unfasten the padlock and lift the lid of the chest. Inside there were big carry-alls of red and white striped canvas, which she vaguely remembered having been used to carry picnic lunches when she was a little girl. Canvas carry-alls with zipper fasteners to hold four hundred thousand dollars in hundred dollar bills! Uncle Paul might be able to tell a hawk from a handsaw, but he was mad north-north-east.

"Did you stop him?" Kay kept her voice low. She had closed the door of the living room but though she thought her uncle had fallen into a light doze, there was a possibility that he might be listening.

She raised her voice a trifle. "How about some coffee?"

In the kitchen Ernest said, frowning, "This is the damnedest thing, darling. I didn't stop the guy; he stopped me. Came out from behind some bushes near the foot of the ravine, signaled for me to pull up, and flashed his credentials. Believe it or not, he's a Treasury man. He looked at my driving license and then searched the car, and I mean searched! When I asked what the hell he was looking for, he gave me a queer sort of look and said, 'You really don't know?' He is convinced that your uncle is hoarding money he has never reported, and he thought I was trying to sneak it out under his eyes."

"It's true, Ernest. Uncle Paul is hoarding. He has just been telling me. He lost everything he had through poor investments and I think it unhinged his mind. His ability to handle money was the one thing that established his superiority over my father, and he couldn't accept the knowledge of his utter failure, couldn't acknowledge the fact that he had been wrong. He never told anyone. In fact, he persuaded Dad to turn over his stocks to him for safe investment and he has converted everything into currency. Ernest, he has four hundred thousand dollars hidden in this house!"

Ernest looked at her blankly, running a hand through his crisp black hair. "My God! This is the weirdest situation I've ever come across. Does he think he can get away with it, particularly now that the government knows what he is doing?"

Kay made a helpless gesture. "I argued with him until I was hoarse and he was so exhausted it frightened me. I told him that he would end by paying a fine that would be a lot worse than taxes, even if he escaped a prison sentence. I told him that it was terribly dangerous to keep so much money in the house, that it was asking for trouble; things like that get around. How did he know that this man wouldn't commit murder to get his hands on that much money? That is, if he really is not a Treasury man, and Uncle Paul simply refuses to believe that he is."

"You know," Ernest said slowly, "your uncle may have something there. I was so staggered by the whole thing that I was caught off base, but now I think about it, I'm inclined to believe there was a strong smell of fish about him."

"So then," Kay went on, "I said, 'Suppose this house catches fire. What would happen then?' That was what finally turned the trick. For a man who is afraid of practically everything, he hadn't, for some reason, considered the possibility of fire."

"What happens now?"

"I persuaded him that he would be safer and more comfortable in my apartment, at least for the time being."

"So we're going to drive him down to New York?"

"Just as soon as we can get going. He's frantic to get away. I'll pack a bag for him now if you can shovel out his car and get it started. That's the real hitch. He absolutely refuses to go in the Cadillac because that man, whoever he is, knows the license number. He won't trust either himself or the money to your car. So I'll have to drive him in that ancient Ford of his with those thrice-accursed canvas bags hidden under a blanket in back."

Seeing how white and shaken she was, Ernest put a comforting arm around her. "There's no excuse for making you drive, feeling the way you do about it, and especially after your frightful experience. I'll talk to the old man, make him see that he'd be safe with me."

She shook her head. "It's no use. I've got as many concessions out of him as I can. He'll leave here and he'll let me take that damned money, but I must admit I won't draw a free breath until I stick it in the bank tomorrow morning."

"I wonder," Ernest said slowly, "whether you are right about that."

"Right!"

"Wait, I'm not arguing about the common sense or the ethics or the legality of the situation. All I'm thinking is that the money he has been hoarding is his chief link with life. A tangible link. Something he can look at and handle. Take that away from him and he might just stop trying. It won't be long, you know; perhaps only a matter of days, scarcely more than a few weeks, judging by what I have seen of him. Then you can handle it as you see fit. Declare it. Pay the fine. Whatever you like."

He saw her troubled expression. "Darling, I don't want to persuade you to do violence to your own standards."

That pernicious, self-righteous word again. Kay couldn't fight it. "Well," she agreed reluctantly, "if you are sure that is best for Uncle Paul. But until the money is safe in the bank where it belongs, I'll feel as though I were roosting on a time bomb."

He grinned at her. "To tell the truth, so will I. We'll probably end by sitting up nights to guard the stuff."

"All I wish," Kay said fervently, "is that I had a Brinks truck instead of Uncle Paul's Ford."

She wished it even more fervently after Ernest had eased his Cadillac over the top of the incline and disappeared. Only when he had gone would Paul Forbes surrender the key to the sea chest. He wasn't going to trust even Ernest with his secret. For a moment Kay was aware of a sense of disloyalty, of betrayal, for having told Ernest; then she remembered that the man on snowshoes had already made the situation clear to him.

The canvas bags were unexpectedly heavy and

she had to drag them out to the car, one at a time, with a sharp lookout for the loiterer. She hoisted them onto the floor in the back of the Ford and covered them with a blanket. If Uncle Paul had to hide the money, why hadn't he chosen something less conspicuous than those bags with their broad red and white stripes? Oh, of course, they were available and he would have had to buy something more suitable.

She reached back to lock the doors of the car. Beside her, bundled to the eyes in a wool scarf, a wool cap pulled over his ears, his hands mittened, Uncle Paul was in a surprisingly cheerful mood. The threat of fire, a danger he had not envisaged, had become so acute that he felt now as though he had escaped catastrophe by the skin of his teeth.

The day was already darkening into night and snow was sifting down lightly. They had agreed that she would wait for Ernest to reach the foot of the hill before she started down. She gripped the wheel, shaken by panic. She couldn't drive a car. Never again. She must have been mad to let Uncle Paul persuade her, but he had been adamant. Ernest's car, he said, wasn't safe. That fellow knew about it, he would stop it and search it. Ernest's job was to lure him away and clear the path for their own undetected departure.

For a moment, Kay, clinging to the wheel, forgot how to start a car, how to stop it. Then she heard the light tap of Ernest's horn and answered it. What you have to do you can do, she told herself, and put the car in gear. A trickle of cold sweat ran down her spine. Suppose there was something wrong with the Ford; no one had driven it in weeks and Ernest had had to work for half an hour to clear it of snow and get it started.

"I was just thinking Kay," Uncle Paul said, "as long as I can't drive again, I'll sell this car when we get to New York. I won't need it there."

She was surprised to discover that she could speak through her tight throat. "You'd have to pay someone to tow it away. How old is it?" Talking, she found helped to drag her attention away from her paralyzing fear.

"Twelve years. Fifteen. Something like that." He sighed. "They don't make them to last any more."

They were on the incline now. She had forgotten how steep it was. She shifted into low gear, but even so the car seemed to be gaining momentum at an alarming rate. At the bottom of the hill Ernest's Cadillac was just turning onto the main road. He'd better get out of the way. At the rate she was traveling she would crash into him.

A man moved onto the road, held up his hand, and Ernest stopped. A sob caught in Kay's throat. "Get out of the way," she whispered to herself. "Get out of the way."

Cautiously she eased her foot on the brake. There was no resistance in the foot pedal. She tried again. The car shot down the incline like a bobsled and just beyond the ravine, Ernest was opening his car door, getting out, the two men were talking, dim figures in the gathering twilight.

"Kay!" Paul shouted. "Kay! Slow up!"

She pulled on the hand brake, slithered to one side, skidded back onto the road, shooting down toward the narrow, slippery bridge and the motionless car.

Below her the two men seemed to be struggling. Through the snow and the failing light she heard Ernest's shout as he started toward her, saw a flurry of movement, and then heard a cry that was cut off abruptly.

"Kay! For God's sake, watch out! Stop!" Uncle Paul's voice had risen to a scream of terror.

"I can't stop." She turned the wheel with all her strength. Better to upset in a snowbank than to continue that suicidal pace and drop twenty feet into the ravine. The Ford swung half off the road, swung back, hit the side of the little bridge. There was a crack, the car shuddered, lurched, seemed to be trying to climb the railing.

CHAPTER 4

The fog lay thick and white. Not a single spot where it had thinned. This, Kay was dimly aware, had happened before, not once but many times, though it was months since the nightmare had recurred.

"John?" she said, but there was no answer. There had been no answer in the other dreams either. "John?"

Something was hurting her head and she put up a hand to stop it.

"Well," a man said cheerfully, "how are you feeling!"

"My head hurts."

"I'll bet it does."

"It was the fog; it came so suddenly, and John —" Her voice rose. "Where is John?"

There was a slight pause and then the man said, "There was no one in the car with you except for your uncle, Miss Forbes."

"But what happened to John?" She tried to sit up and was pushed back by gentle hands. "Who are you?"

"I'm Dr. Grantling. Perhaps you don't remember me. Last summer, when you were visiting your uncle, you came to consult me about your headaches. You've had a narrow escape from death, young lady. I don't suppose you remember how it happened."

"There was a fog and then all the cars piled up."

"That was a different accident, one that happened more than a year ago. Don't worry about it. Just rest."

"Doesn't she remember anything?" a woman asked.

"She may in time."

"According to Mrs. Brundle there was always a queer streak in the Forbes family. She says even as a child Miss Forbes was always imagining the craziest things, that she'd gone for a walk with a unicorn, stuff like that."

"When we can get her to the hospital I'll want some X-rays. So far as I can tell, there is nothing wrong except for a mild concussion and shock, but this is the second crackup she has been involved in and I never knew the extent of the damage done the first time. I heard vague rumors about extensive brain injury and she had severe headaches long after she should have been well."

"Accident-prone," the woman suggested.

"Well —" The doctor did not pursue the idea. "What I didn't like was that morbid sense of guilt she carried for the other accident. Felt she had killed the man she was going to marry."

"I don't envy you the job of telling her about this one."

The words were a meaningless blur. Something was struggling in Kay's mind, something she had to remember. The fog was rolling away now. She recalled the runaway car, the crash, Uncle Paul's scream. And Uncle Paul was dead. Like John. Like — what was it she had to remember? She sat upright, resisting the doctor's restraining hands. His finger rested on her racing pulse and then she felt the prick of a needle.

She was awakened by the barking of a dog, became aware of a white-clad woman beside a shaded lamp, sitting bolt upright as though straining to hear. She was in her room at Uncle Paul's and something had happened. Before she could capture the elusive memory, she slept again.

Next time she opened her eyes the room was filled with sunlight. The door opened and a woman came in, a thin woman with nervous lips and anxious eyes.

"I am Mrs. Prescott, your nurse." She thrust a thermometer under Kay's tongue, took her pulse. "I guess you're going to be all right now. Doctor will be so pleased." A car door slammed and the dog set up a frenzied barking. "That will be Doctor now."

"Whose dog is making that row?"

"He's my shepherd. I go on night duty and some of these places are isolated. Monarch is a fine watchdog. When he's around, I'm never nervous."

"I should think the patients would be. I never heard such a racket."

The nurse gave her a placating look. "I hope

you won't complain to Doctor. Monarch has never been noisy before. I don't know what gets into him here. He can't seem to settle down at night. Something about the house upsets him, I guess." She cast a sidewise look at Kay. "I sure was grateful for all those bolts and chains. Never saw a house so well guarded."

When Kay made no reply, she said tentatively. "I couldn't help wondering if maybe your uncle was afraid of something."

Kay was still silent.

Hearing a series of explosions, the nurse said in a tone of relief, "That will be Mrs. Brundle. She spells me in the mornings while I get some sleep. But I'll be right across the hall if I'm needed. I'll just have a word with Doctor and then go beddy-bye." She tittered and went out, closing the door behind her casually, as though absentmindedly.

Kay heard the murmur of voices and then Dr. Grantling came in. "Hello, there. You look more like yourself now." He sat down beside the bed, beaming at her, but Kay got the impression that he was ill at ease. "Has Mrs. Prescott been taking good care of you?"

"I don't really know. I seem to have slept for a long time."

"Best thing in the world for you." Had the doctor always been as hearty as this? "Sleep is a great healer. We were lucky to get a nurse. Always a shortage in small communities, you know."

"How long have I been here?"

"You were unconscious for five days but you are out of the woods now."

"What happened to Uncle Paul Doctor?" When he made no immediate reply, she said steadily, "He's dead, isn't he? I killed him."

"Now, Miss Forbes, don't get worked up. The old man is dead, yes. But he died of heart failure as a result of shock and fright. It was only a matter of a short time at best. I'd been treating him for weeks. You must not blame yourself for what happened. That's a dangerous hill, I've always said so, and on an unsanded road you couldn't have prevented it. You struck the other car on the bridge and sent it over into the ravine."

Kay remembered the Ford crashing into the railing on the bridge. Ernest's car had been on the other side of the bridge, turned toward the main road. She hadn't struck it. It couldn't have gone into the ravine. Not possibly. She started to tell the doctor so, saw him watching her intently. Something in his expression gave her the first intimation of warning, the first stirring of fear.

"Ernest?" she asked at length.

"The drop is twenty feet," he reminded her, "and the car caught on fire."

Kay turned her face to the wall, and after a time the doctor went out of the room. There seemed to be no feeling at all, not pain, not grief, just a kind of numbness. She had killed them all: John and Uncle Paul and Ernest. She repeated the words to herself. Three men were dead because of her. Ernest with his gaiety, his confidence, his laughter, his vigorous health; Ernest charred in the big Cadillac at the bottom of the ravine. She flung her arm over her eyes as though to shut out the unbearable — and suddenly she was alert.

"But it didn't happen that way," she said aloud.

It was unfortunate that Mrs. Brundle heard her talking to herself. The housekeeper came creaking and wheezing into the room, breathless from climbing the steep stairs. She gave Kay a startled look.

"Come to yourself, have you? We was beginning to worry, that crack on the head and all. Still I guess you was lucky at that. Like I was telling poor Nelly last night, the way you just lay there was a caution. Still the doctor says it's nature's way of healing."

She propped pillows behind Kay, slid a tray onto her lap. "Orange juice and tea and a soft-boiled egg. If that sets all right, you'll get something more nourishing for your dinner. I'll leave it for Mrs. Prescott to serve. I got to go early because I have a new lodger and I want him to taste a real New England boiled dinner. He's never ate one before, if you can imagine! Nelly can keep an eye on it until I get home."

She sat down heavily and mopped her face. "My lodger's taken quite a shine to Nelly. They get along fine. The poor man is waiting for a cataract operation and can't see good, so Nelly reads to him."

Poor Nelly, Kay thought. For five years Mrs. Brundle had been taking in male lodgers and providing them with what was probably the best-cooked food in Connecticut, hoping that one of them would be attracted to Nelly. Each time she managed to convince herself, in the face of over-whelming evidence of indifference, that the man was interested in her daughter. As a rule, two months was par for the course. After that, in sheer self-preservation, the lodger moved out.

"Mr. Worth looks like he'd be permanent," Mrs. Brundle said, hope springing eternal in her breast. "Not like the last one. Just up and left without notice. Of course, a photographer is kind of a footloose fellow, say what you will, going around taking pictures of scenic spots. No future in that. Nelly tried real hard to help him, wanted to learn about developing and all like that, but he didn't seem —" She sighed.

Kay sipped tea, dipped a spoon in the egg. "Mrs. Brundle, I'd like to know what happened." She saw the wariness in the housekeeper's face and added with shameless flattery, "There's no one but you who could tell me. You're such an old friend and so understanding. It happened so fast that I'm sort of confused. I don't seem to remember."

After a sharp look the housekeeper relaxed. "Well, you skidded, of course. And no one blames you. Get that in your head, Kay. Not a soul. I been complaining about that road all winter and after the troopers saw it — well, they raised ructions, I can tell you. Right now it's the best-sanded road around here. Anyhow, you skidded into the Cadillac. The troopers said there were no brakes on the Ford, that the car shouldn't have been allowed on the road, though it was all right last time your uncle drove it. No one could figure out why you was using two cars anyhow." She waited for an answer that was not forthcoming.

"Well, anyhow, someone on the main road heard the crash and reported it. By the time the troopers got there the Cadillac had pretty well burned out. They brought you up here. The hospital is overcrowded and you didn't seem much hurt except — your head —" Her voice trailed off.

Kay waited until she was under control. "Tell me about Uncle Paul."

"They didn't hold up the services, of course, because there's no other Forbeses anyhow, except you, and you couldn't of gone anyhow. He's in the family plot. He looked real nice, Kay, real natural. There was a lot of flowers and just about everyone turned out for the funeral, and the service was lovely, just lovely. You'd have thought everyone liked him."

"And Ernest?" Kay said steadily.

"Well, they couldn't find out anything about him, about his folks, I mean, and all that. I said you was engaged to marry him, so they went ahead — a double funeral, you know — and put him in your family plot, too. We thought you'd like it that way."

Like it. Kay pushed away the tray. "You were all very kind." She spoke casually. "By the way, where are the canvas bags that were in the Ford?"

"There was nothing in the Ford except for an old blanket. We thought you'd taken it in case your uncle felt the cold. Though why you was taking him anywheres in a storm like that and in his condition no one could rightly figure out."

"We were taking him away because he wasn't safe in this house. And we've got to find those canvas bags; there were hundreds of thousands of dollars in them, everything Uncle Paul had. And," Kay heard her voice rise treacherously but she could not control it. "I didn't hit the Cadillac. I wasn't near it. Ernest was deliberately murdered. I saw it happen! I could identify the man who killed him. I want you to call the troopers right now, Mrs. Brundle."

Mrs. Brundle gave her an alarmed glance, picked up the tray and went out of the room as though she were escaping. Kay heard her on the telephone, but it was not the troopers she summoned, it was Dr. Grantling.

All the rest of the morning Mrs. Brundle moved around the house at a kind of slow bustle, but she kept out of Kay's room, almost as though she were afraid of her. Which was absurd. At length Kay heard the dog barking and then voices

59

downstairs, the doctor's carefully raised so it would carry.

• "Now you just run along, Mrs. Brundle. I know you have plenty to do at home and the young lady and I can manage until Mrs. Prescott wakes up."

He came into the room. "Well, well," he boomed, "you're looking better every hour. Nothing like rest. Nature knows more than all the doctors." He laughed heartily. "I was just telling Mrs. Brundle we'd have a nice chat until Mrs. Prescott gets back on the job. She's been staying right here in the house, you know, in case you needed her."

"I won't need her long. I'd like to get back to New York as soon as possible."

"Now don't rush things. You'd be wise to take it easy for a while. Matter of fact, I've made a tentative reservation for you at Fenwick for next week. They'll put you on your feet in no time."

"Fenwick!" The place was euphemistically called a rest home, but it was generally known to be an expensive retreat for drug addicts, alcoholics, and people suffering from what they preferred to call nervous disorders. "But I'm not crazy!"

"Of course you aren't," he agreed too heartily. "Now you aren't to worry about a thing. An old friend has come up to shoulder all your worries. Mr. Stoddard." He waited to see a look of pleasure on her face, failed to find anything but extreme surprise.

"Malcolm Stoddard? He was my father's friend, but I barely know the man. Why is he here?"

"I'll let him tell you." Dr. Grantling went out and the door closed. After a few minutes Malcolm Stoddard followed his light tap on the door.

He had not, Kay thought, changed at all. He did not seem to have aged, though it was years since she had encountered him. Tall, slim, elegant, fastidious, he looked at sixty much as he had done at fifty.

He took her hand. "Well, Kay, the doctor gives me good news of you. He says you'll be able to leave here in another week." He pulled up a chair and sat looking at her, a polite smile on his lips, wariness in his eyes. It was a look she was beginning to watch for, to fear.

"You know what happened?" she asked cautiously.

He nodded with becoming gravity and sorrow. "Poor Paul! Still, take it all in all, not a bad way to go. Quick and painless. And, at best, he had so short a time left, Kay."

"It was my fault. I killed him."

He moved a hand in sudden alarm. "Now, now, don't get excited."

"Please," she wiped away the tears of weakness impatiently, "don't let them tell you there is anything wrong with my mind. I don't mean that I actually killed him; but I insisted on his leaving the house where, for all I know, he might have been safe. And then the brakes failed. And then —"

"The accident may have precipitated the end by a few days, but that is all. Nothing to concern you, believe me. Remember that he was an old man, a doomed man."

"But Ernest wasn't. He was young and he was healthy. He should have had a whole lifetime ahead if I hadn't let him come up with me and dragged him into this —" She was beginning to shake.

"That was Ernest Billings? Mrs. Brundle, who made the identification, says you were planning to marry him. I am very sorry, Kay. You have my deepest sympathy. You know about the funeral arrangements, of course. It was decided to go ahead, though we regretted being unable to reach Mr. Billing's family. We put an announcement in the papers but there was no response."

"He didn't have any family. Originally he came from Georgia, but he told me there was no one left."

"What about his job? Someone should notify his employers."

"I don't know who he worked for," Kay said, and remembered Ernest telling her, "You are my job now."

There was rather an uncomfortable pause, then he said noncommittally, "You were planning to marry this man without knowing anything about him?"

"I knew the kind of person he was and that's all that mattered."

"Are you acquainted with any of his friends?"

She shook her head.

"You had just met him, I take it."

She described their meeting three months earlier and was perfectly aware that he was docketing the information in his orderly and fastidious mind as a pickup.

"And that's all you know about him?"

"Oh, what difference —" she began.

"In contemporary civilization a man can't just disappear," he pointed out with a disciplined patience that underlined her own irritability. "He must have a place to live; he must have a bank account, in which the income-tax people are interested. He must have left some kind of estate. And he must, in all probability, have been working somewhere, at something."

"I think he worked for the government, something hush-hush," Kay said, and she repeated Ernest's comment about the mission. "He obviously didn't want me to ask questions because it was highly confidential, but I suppose that won't matter now."

"He was out of the country six months ago and he told you, 'Say it was a mission but don't say it too loud.' " Stoddard brightened. "That should give us a lead. I'll set inquiries going at once." When she made no comment, he said, "That's what you want, isn't it?" He repeated more insistently, "Isn't it?"

"Whatever you think best. All I've done so far is harm."

"No one blames you for the accident, Kay. But the troopers did wonder — I've been at the barracks to have a little talk with them — why Paul was leaving the house in his condition and in a storm, and why you were using two cars."

"Uncle Paul was afraid to drive with Ernest because the man knew his car. Ernest was to draw him off so we could get away in the Ford."

Stoddard looked at her searchingly. "And why did you need to get away?"

She looked up to find him watching her and she slid her telltale hands under the blanket to conceal their shaking. "Uncle Paul was afraid of fire. He had never thought of the possibility of fire before. He couldn't wait to leave."

"And why fire? Why, after — how long is it — nearly two hundred years that this house has stood?"

"Because he had four hundred thousand dollars in currency he was hoarding in this house, Mr. Stoddard. He lost everything he had on the market and I think it affected him mentally. He took over Dad's stocks and converted them into currency. He hadn't even paid income taxes. He had all that money in two big red and white striped canvas bags in that old sea chest in the hall."

"I see." She did not hear the warning in his voice. "Rather — inadequate protection, wouldn't you say?"

"It was quite mad, of course," she agreed readily. "That's why I urged him to leave. Anyhow, he was terrified of this house and of the man who had been hanging around, the one who claimed to be a Treasury agent. So I persuaded him to go, and now both he and Ernest are dead."

"What do you remember of the accident?" When she had told him, he said, "I wonder if you are aware that your account does not agree in a single particular with the report made by the troopers."

"I'm beginning to," she said grimly. "Just the same, I never struck the Cadillac. I wasn't near it. That was sent into the ravine by the man who stopped the car; the man who killed Ernest."

"My dear girl!"

Kay flung out a hand in pleading. "Please try to believe me, Mr. Stoddard. Give me the benefit of the doubt. Check my story. Check Uncle Paul's estate and my father's." She was sitting bolt upright now. "Look at the chains and locks and bolts on this house. I didn't put them there. Uncle Paul did. Why do you think he had them installed? Because he was afraid. That's why he sent for me, to protect him, he said."

Stoddard pushed back his chair. "I'm afraid I have tired you and I mustn't do that. The doctor doesn't want you to overdo. We'll have to arrange for you to get a proper rest."

"You don't believe me, do you?"

"You've had a bad accident, Kay, and a severe

shock. You have been confused. They tell me you thought at first the accident happened during a heavy fog."

"That's true, but I remember now."

"You are quite sure you haven't imagined all this fantastic story about theft and murder?"

"Mr. Stoddard, if you authorize Dr. Grantling to send me to Fenwick, that will be on my record always. No one will ever believe this story, will they? Don't let him do it. Please! Give me time to prove to you that I am sane. If I do anything peculiar, then, of course, you'd be justified. But first try to help me. Look for that man with the pointed lip. I saw him. I could identify him. I intend to identify him. Somewhere that man has the money he stole; somewhere he is free to kill again. Do you think that is right? If you send me to Fenwick now, no one would ever accept my testimony as being trustworthy, even if I could produce the murderer."

For a long time Stoddard was silent. Then he said, "We won't hurry things. I'll talk to the doctor and have him cancel the reservation at Fenwick. Temporarily. I'll look into Paul's affairs and your father's. If you are right about the money having disappeared, you wouldn't be able to afford Fenwick, anyhow. I'm afraid you are going to find yourself hard up unless you have other resources."

"I have a co-operative apartment in New York and about three thousand dollars in the bank. That's all. I am sure I can sell the apartment without any difficulty and I'll put this house on the market. There's no reason why I can't get a job that would keep me. Other women do it every day, even when they have no training."

He seemed to be relieved by her attitude, and particularly by her clear summary of the situation. "Well, I must get back to New York. I'll investigate your financial position and see what I can do about selling this place and your New York apartment. You'll need quite a bit of ready cash to support you until you are well enough to work." He patted her hand, started toward the door, wheeled around. "Kay."

"Yes."

"You'd be wiser, I think, not to go about proclaiming that you could identify this man."

"Why?" she asked in surprise.

"Sometimes it isn't healthy to know a murderer."

CHAPTER 5

Apparently Kay had made more of an impression than she had dared to hope on Malcolm Stoddard, for nothing more was said about a sojourn at Fenwick. Of course, the decision might have been influenced by the fact that she lacked the funds to pay for it. Cushioned isolation — or insulation — from the difficulties of being an adult comes high.

However, Dr. Grantling insisted on her remaining at the Forbes house for at least ten more days before returning to New York; Mrs. Prescott, he said, was to remain with her. Kay was aware that the doctor was not satisfied with her mental condition, but she thought it wiser not to protest. She had gained her chief point and for the rest she would have to rely on time — and a little luck.

Already she had learned to check her impulsive tongue, to think twice before she spoke. Before she could be free to embark on the course she had set herself, she would have to allay suspicion. None the less, she did not require the nurse's attentions, and the barking of Monarch awakened her every night. Mrs. Prescott insisted on remaining in Kay's room, not so much, Kay thought, to provide protection as to receive it.

She would sit bolt upright in her chair and she developed an unnerving habit of looking swiftly over her shoulder. She was quite frankly terrified of going downstairs in the dark and she kept lights burning in every room as well as the outside floodlight. From the village below, the house on the hill must seem to be lighted up like a Christmas tree.

"Your Florence Nightingale is about as soothing to have around as a poltergeist," Kay informed the doctor, "and that damned dog of hers ought to be muzzled."

"She's a nervous woman."

"You're telling me!"

"She says the dog never acted like this before. Something about the house upsets it."

"The old family ghost, no doubt."

He laughed. "Well, it's a cinch nothing else could get past those bolts and chains." He added, "How are the headaches?" It was a question he had a habit of slipping unobtrusively into the conversation.

"Much better," Kay lied. Pain stabbed savagely through her head, bound her forehead in an iron band, but she dared not admit it.

There were moments when she wondered whether the doctor was right, whether there was some serious injury to her brain. She forced down her panic. She was all right, she told herself fiercely. Before she could permit herself to face the implications of that crippling pain, there was a job to be done. She was going to find and expose Ernest's murderer, not only as a matter of justice but because it was the only way in which she could free herself of the suspicions mounting around her that the whole story was the figment of a diseased mind.

"How soon will you let me go?" she asked. That was on the tenth day after the accident.

"Five more days. Unless, of course, there are complications."

There weren't, she determined, going to be any complications that he could detect. A few bad moments occurred but fortunately when she was alone. The first was when she was allowed to get out of bed. She blacked out but, by the time Mrs. Brundle entered her room, she was sitting on the side of the bed, white-faced but upright. The second was when she ventured down the steep stairs, fighting an almost irresistible impulse to plunge forward on her face.

Luckily she had recovered when the telephone rang. Malcolm Stoddard was speaking from New York.

"Kay, I have some good news for you. An excellent offer to rent your studio up there for three months. I've talked to the local authorities and they'll let you go ahead in the somewhat peculiar circumstances."

"What do you mean?"

"Well, Paul's estate has not been settled, of course. In fact, his records are in a state of unbelievable chaos. But everyone in your community knows the Forbeses — at one time they owned the entire township — and there is no hitch about renting. I strongly advise you to accept the offer. You couldn't get a finer or more reliable tenant. Deke Ransom, no less." He was as triumphant as an amateur at *léger de main* pulling a rabbit out of a hat.

"Deke Ransom? The man who does the Talking Portraits?"

"That's the one. He'd like to move in immediately, if that's all right with you."

"But I understood that he traveled all the time, getting his interviews with famous people."

"He wants to take a kind of sabbatical and devote himself to serious painting for a few months."

"Well, if you think so."

"Good. I'll set it up at once."

"Mr. Stoddard, you've really been checking on Uncle Paul's estate, haven't you?"

"Trying to. That is — trying to."

"Do you believe me now?"

"We'll discuss all that when you come to New York. Dr. Grantling tells me you'll probably be able to make the trip before the end of the week if all goes well."

"All," she assured him, "will go well. Have you found out anything about Ernest?"

"That's developed into rather an odd situation, Kay. We'll talk about it when I see you." He broke the connection before she could ask further questions.

When she had left the telephone, she stood

staring out of the window. A spring thaw had routed the sullen winter and melted the snow; water ran noisily in a brook behind the studio. The trees were still stark, but a hardy crocus had thrust up its fragile head on the lawn.

"I've got to get back home early," Mrs. Brundle said. "My lodger likes my blueberry pie and I promised him one for his supper. It's a good thing I put up all those quarts of blueberries last year. Poor Nelly has a heavy hand with pastry, but lately she's been trying real hard. When you're feeling better, I hope you'll come and visit with Nelly."

"As soon as the doctor lets me out of here, I'll have to go to New York on business. Then I'll come back to live until the estate is settled and I can sell the house."

"Live here alone?"

"Why not? Uncle Paul did."

"He wasn't in his right mind, if you ask me," Mrs. Brundle said bluntly. "It's no place for you to stay by yourself. Mrs. Prescott says the house gives her the fidgets at night. And Monarch, too."

"She'd have the fidgets wherever she was," Kay retorted. "That dog of hers is enough to drive anyone crazy." She would have liked to take back the words.

"A good watchdog is what you need," Mrs. Brundle said, after one of those queer searching looks to which Kay was becoming accustomed if not reconciled. "Living here alone. It's not safe.

72

If the Hammonds had come back, you'd at least have someone to call. You think it over."

"Oh, I nearly forgot; I won't be alone, Mr. Stoddard has rented the studio to a Mr. Ransom who'll be coming up right away. In a few days, he said. Tomorrow you had better let the work here go and start getting the studio in shape for him."

"It will need a real good turnout after so long. No one has used the place in years. Probably dust and spiders all over it."

"I don't know about spiders, but there are rats in the storeroom. You'd better set some traps."

"I'll do my work and I'll clean up the place real good, but I won't have anything to do with rats. Nasty, dangerous things. They can stay in the storeroom for all of me, or the new tenant can get rid of them for himself."

Kay shrugged. "Well, all I hope is that he won't mind. I certainly don't want to drive him away. The rent will be a godsend until I am able to work."

"It was true, then," Mrs. Brundle said in surprise, "what you said. Your uncle's money is gone."

"Yes, it's gone."

"No wonder you are half out of your mind," Mrs. Brundle stopped herself with an audible gasp. "All I mean was the worrying. I must say you look like the wrath of God, Kay. Your eyes are like black holes in a piece of dough, and no flesh on you to speak of. You ought to watch yourself. You don't want to get pneumonia in your condition."

The day her new tenant was to move in Kay arranged to go to New York. She had paid off Mrs. Prescott and they parted with mutual relief. In her usual bracing manner the nurse's last remark was, "Now don't overdo. You look just awful, Miss Forbes."

The original plan had been for Mrs. Brundle to admit the tenant on his arrival. "That will give me a chance," she explained, "to find out if he needs a cleaning woman. Anyways, I'd like to size him up for myself. It don't seem proper, you living alone up here with a strange man on the place. You know how people talk."

But this plan had to be abandoned when it appeared that the local taxi driver would be unable to take Miss Forbes to the train. Mrs. Brundle looked rather queer when she came away from the telephone.

"Tell you what," she said with an uncharacteristic heartiness that reminded Kay of Dr. Grantling's manner of dealing with her, "I'll drive you down to the station myself in the jeep."

"You mean," Kay said incredulously, "the taxi driver is afraid of me?"

"Well," the housekeeper was uncomfortable, "you know how things get around. That story of yours about your young man being murdered — people always said there was a queer streak in the Forbeses."

Kay turned away numbly, toiled up the stairs

to her room. Pain stabbed jaggedly through her head. A queer streak. A queer streak. For a long moment she stared at herself in the mirror. She had never looked worse in her life, she conceded. Eyes like black holes in a piece of dough. Eyes that were too sunken and too bright. A queer streak. Because she said that Ernest had been murdered.

Ernest. She could almost feel his presence beside her, his immense vitality, his assurance, the quality that had given her such comfort. Was that what she had been seeking, she wondered in a moment of insight, someone to be strength and support, someone to provide the assurance she lacked, someone to laugh away her corroding sense of guilt? Was it possible that it had been only her need that had made her promise to marry him? The savage pain racked her skull and the iron band tightened around her forehead. Walking softly so as not to jar her head, she began to prepare for town.

She had a long and disillusioning session with her mirror. If she were to succeed in her project, she must convince Malcolm Stoddard that she was a completely normal woman, that she did not suffer from aberrations. Never, even in preparation for an important evening, had she spent so much time in self-study, done so much experimenting with her hair, with make-up. On the whole, she was satisfied. A cunning use of cosmetics had obliterated the hollows under her eyes, her cheeks had a healthy glow, she applied lipstick lavishly. She was, she realized in surprised relief, temporarily free from the headache.

In an exquisitely cut gray Parisian suit, a sable cape over her shoulders, a small hat perched on her dark hair, she looked more like the Kay Forbes of a month ago. She took a final look in the mirror. Whatever happens, she warned herself, think before you speak. Don't panic. But in spite of herself, as she went downstairs, she heard in her ears the mocking words, "There's a queer streak."

Mrs. Brundle, squeezed by some miracle behind the wheel of the jeep, gave her an appraising look. "Well," she exclaimed as Kay climbed in beside her, "you're more like yourself. Nelly always thought you was the Cleopatra type; sort of lush, if you know what I mean; but I could never see it myself. Right now, though, you're really something."

Kay, about to disclaim any ambition to play Cleopatra, found herself concentrating fiercely on maintaining self-control.

The jeep had topped the incline, started down. Kay shut her eyes. Don't look, she told herself. Don't look. But of course she did look. She couldn't help it. The jeep was moving slowly, well under control. Far below she could hear water rushing in the ravine. The road was clear. Then, beyond the bridge, she saw a car turning off the highway. It was all happening again.

"Look out!" she screamed.

The wheel jerked in Mrs. Brundle's hands,

then she sounded her horn in warning and continued down the hill at a sedate pace. The other car had stopped, backed, pulled to one side.

"You didn't ought to have done that," Mrs. Brundle scolded. "I mighta lost control. You're downright hysterical, Kay."

"I'm sorry." Kay sat with her hands clenched, her heart pounding, breath coming in rasping gasps.

Mrs. Brundle stopped the jeep. "You the new tenant?"

There were three people in the car, a young man and a girl on the front seat, a man alone in back. It was the latter who spoke.

"I am Deke Ransom."

Mrs. Brundle fished in her pocket. "This key unlocks the studio. I'll be back in an hour in case you need any help."

"Thank you," the man's voice was pleasant, "but I have my own couple." For a moment his eyes rested on Kay, then returned to the housekeeper. Kay, still struggling to control her breathing, did not turn her head. At his signal the cream-colored Pontiac turned, crossed the bridge, started up the hill.

"Looks like a nice steady sort of fellow," Mrs. Brundle commented. "Seems to me I've seen him somewhere, or at least his picture. His own couple. Well, he might still want a cleaning woman. That girl didn't look to me as though she was up to much, and that's a fact. Nelly will be interested. Poor Nelly likes to hear about new people. She's so cut off. That's what I like about my lodger, Mr. Worth. He's real companionable. Talks to Nelly by the hour. And obliging, I can tell you. Like he says, he can't see much, but there's nothing wrong with the rest of him. Always running errands and things like that." She cast an uneasy look at Kay. "You feeling all right now?"

"Yes, it was just as though it were happening all over again."

"Well, it didn't," Mrs. Brundle said comfortably. "But I can tell you one thing, Kay. Your tenant may be all right, but I don't think much of that couple of his, and that's a fact. The man didn't act like a servant, if you know what I mean. He had — watching eyes. And the girl, pretty enough in a washed-out way, but I'll bet she can't stand up to housework and she's no cook. I know a good cook when I see one. And another thing, that girl takes dope of some kind."

"Oh, surely not!"

"I saw the same thing when I did for old Mrs. Harling. Remember her? Toward the end she took as many as four sleeping pills a night and she had that same blind look in her eyes.

"Well," she added cheerfully as she drove up at the station, "enjoy yourself and don't worry about a thing!"

CHAPTER 6

The manager of the Fifth Avenue apartment was discreetly sorry to hear that Miss Forbes had suffered a loss in her family. He could speak for all the tenants in expressing his regret that she was going to leave them, but there would be no problem about selling the apartment. There was a gratifyingly long list of potential buyers. He could assure her that the transfer would be put through at once. The price provided an agreeable surprise. Kay was amused to find that her father's investments should prove to have been so much sounder than his brother's.

When she had packed her clothes and personal things, she arranged for the furniture to be stored. It was extraordinary to discover how quickly one could make a permanent break with a way of life. Adjustment to change might, she thought, be easier if there were more trouble involved. For the last time she stood looking at the stupendous view.

Three weeks ago, when she had stood at this window, Ernest had been with her, his hands resting on her shoulders. There had been no nightmare then, only Uncle Paul's frightened summons and Ernest's fortifying presence. There had been something ahead. Now all that was gone. Ernest and Uncle Paul and — well, no sense in being dishonest about it — the money. Not that it had the same value as two human lives, but it was uncomfortably essential.

The doorman's whistle summoned a taxi and Kay gave the address of Ernest's apartment. There might be a possibility of learning something about him and his background. Perhaps there would be a photograph, at least a snapshot. In any case, it was the only starting point she had.

Somehow, some way, she had to prove that she was not responsible for Ernest's death. There could be no peace for her until she had done so, no real assurance that the whole tragic, ugly situation was not something conjured up by an over imaginative or disturbed mind.

She was aware of the obstacles she faced. The police did not believe her. Dr. Grantling did not believe her. Mrs. Brundle's comments about "a queer streak" were such common knowledge in the village that the taxi driver was afraid of her. Malcolm Stoddard had been frankly incredulous. One mistake, one action that could be termed eccentric, and she would find herself in Fenwick. And that meant that even when she was released, her story would have no credibility.

There were moments when she was on the verge of panic, moments when the agonizing headaches recurred, when her courage was shaken, but her determination remained. She would find and expose the man who had murdered Ernest.

According to the cards over the bells in the entrance hall of the building where he had lived, the owner occupied the fourth floor. The stairs proved to be heavy going and she found herself hanging onto the banister and pulling herself up the last flight. Her knees were shaking and she was out of breath.

The woman who opened the door was about sixty, dressed in a tailored suit, with a rather severe face and keen eyes, which summed Kay up in a sharp glance. Then she stretched out an unexpectedly strong hand and drew the girl into her living room, eased her into a chair. As Kay started to speak, she said, "Wait until you catch your breath. Those stairs are difficult when you aren't accustomed to them," another look, "or when you have been ill."

For a moment she looked down at Kay in concern and then she went out of the room. When her heart had steadied and her breathing had slowed down, Kay glanced around her. On this floor the rooms had a lower ceiling but the same lovely proportions as those in Ernest's apartment. The place was filled with antiques. Apparently, as she had been forced to rent more and more of her house, the owner had brought her cherished belongings with her.

There was a faint tinkle of china and the woman came in with a tray holding a pot of tea, lemon, and sugar. She set it on a small table beside Kay with a fragile cup and saucer.

"Drink that before you try to talk."

Kay recalled now that she had forgotten to eat lunch and her hostess brought a toasted muffin dripping with butter.

"You look better," she said when Kay had finished. When she smiled, her rather severe face became charming. "You have been ill, haven't you?"

"I was in an accident. The reason I came here, Mrs. —"

"Willows. An absurd name, isn't it?"

"Mrs. Willows. I am Kay Forbes. I was engaged to be married to Ernest Billings."

Something flickered over Mrs. Willows's face. Suspicion? Caution? She made no comment at all.

"He was killed two weeks ago."

Mrs. Willows's expression changed from one of bland discretion to one of shock. "Killed? Oh, my dear child!"

"There was an automobile accident on an icy road." Kay was speaking carefully now. "The police think my car rammed his. It was found in the ravine. It had — burned out."

"What a dreadful thing! I am terribly sorry."

"So, as soon as the doctor would give me permission, I wanted to come here."

Again the odd expression was on Mrs. Willows's face. "You've been here before?"

"Only once. The night before we went up to Connecticut. I came in for a few minutes."

Mrs. Willows smiled. "I wondered how anyone could possibly be here without my second-floor tenant, Mr. Frazer, knowing about it, and yet they say that women are the gossips! He never misses any—" She broke off. "Miss Forbes, did you say Mr. Billings was — that he died two weeks ago?"

Kay nodded.

"Then who was in his apartment last week?" When Kay stared in bewilderment, she went on, "Mr. Frazer was quite annoyed about it. He said Mr. Billings seemed to be moving furniture around half the night. I thought myself —" Mrs. Willows stopped abruptly. Then she got to her feet. "This will have to be looked into. Do you feel like — would you mind going down to the apartment?"

"That's why I came," Kay reminded her.

The older woman's eyes rested searchingly on her face. "There's nothing of his left there, you know."

"Nothing of his? You mean everything was moved out in the night?"

"Oh, no. None of the furniture belonged to him. Mr. Billings sublet the first floor three months ago. The furnishings belong to my regular tenant who went abroad on business."

"But Ernest's clothes, his —" Kay was bewildered.

"Every scrap of his personal belongings has been removed. I suspected — I'm ashamed now, knowing of his tragic death — that he had simply cleared out in the middle of the night."

Kay flared into anger. "How could you possibly believe that of a man like Ernest?"

"Don't mistake me, Miss Forbes. I thought he was charming. He impressed me as being a highly responsible person."

"Then what on earth made you suspect him?"

"Nothing at all," Mrs. Willows said readily. "It was more a case," and she smiled, again softening her expression, "of the strange behavior of the dog in the night. He did nothing, if you remember. Once I have accepted a tenant, I don't check up on him. Please believe that. But I couldn't help noticing that Mr. Billings never received any mail. Mr. Frazer says he never got a telephone call — he can hear the phone ring in his apartment and my regular tenant got a great many calls, which annoyed him. And, again according to Mr. Frazer, he had no visitors."

"But what's wrong —" Kay began helplessly.

"It's rather an odd way for a young man to live, that's all. Oddly secretive."

But he had a secretive job, Kay started to say, and thought better of it.

"And there was another rather unusual thing," Mrs. Willows was speaking more slowly now, "he paid me in traveler's checks when he took over that sublease."

In his job he probably needed them, Kay thought, wishing she could state openly what Ernest's job was. For the first time she realized how difficult his own position must have been.

Mrs. Willows led the way down the stairs, walking briskly and lightly, carrying herself like a young woman, while Kay followed more slowly, her head pounding with the jar of every step.

Mrs. Willows unlocked the door of Ernest's apartment and then switched on the lights. "Ground floors are always dark in New York."

Kay looked around. It was exactly as it had been the night she had come here with Ernest. Mrs. Willows showed her the bedroom, bathroom, and kitchenette. There were no clothes in the closet, nothing in the dresser drawers, no signs to indicate that Ernest had ever been here, except in the small kitchen. On the drainboard beside the sink there were two small glasses.

"We had some orange juice that night," Kay said huskily. "And I remember him telling me he hadn't stopped for breakfast the next morning. It's almost as though no one had been here."

"Except the man — or whoever it was — who disturbed Mr. Frazer in the night last week. I'm going to report this to the police and have the locks changed. Though I don't understand — that's a real Braque on the wall and my tenant left all his silver. I don't understand."

"Neither do I, but I intend to find out."

"Is there anything else I can tell you or show you?"

Kay shook her head.

"Then I'll turn out the lights in the kitchen and bedroom."

While Kay waited for Mrs. Willows to come

back, she opened her handbag in an automatic search for lipstick. The lipstick fell on the carpet and rolled under the edge of the couch. She bent over, groped and picked up the lipstick and something else. She opened her hand, saw the enameled cuff link with an odd design. That must be the one Ernest had lost. It was all she had of him. She slipped it into her handbag.

As she walked down the street — and she felt the need of getting some exercise, getting some order into her thoughts before she met Malcolm Stoddard — Kay tried to cope with the senseless enigma of the disappearance of Ernest's belongings from his apartment a week after his death.

That it was only Ernest who had interested the night visitor was made clear by the fact that neither a valuable painting nor expensive silver had been touched. One thing troubled her vaguely. True, Ernest had not stated outright that the furnishings were his, but he had implied it. He had sublet the apartment three months ago; about the time, then, when they had met at a charity performance at the theater. And behind that there was a blank wall.

Say it was a mission. The words came back to her with a flood of relief. Of course, he held some hush-hush government job. It was undoubtedly one of his colleagues who had taken care to remove all his effects from the apartment. But why, then, hadn't it been done openly? Why hadn't Mrs. Willows been informed that her tenant was dead? Surely that was the kind thing to do; the obvious thing, too, if it was desirable to forestall any search for him.

And who else knew of his death? True, Mr. Stoddard had put an announcement in the papers, but there had been no accompanying picture. So far as Kay was aware, no picture of Ernest existed.

Engrossed in her thoughts, it was not until she reached Thirty-fourth Street that Kay began to feel that she was being followed. The impression was so strong that she stopped abruptly and turned to look at the people behind her. No one paid her the slightest attention. They simply went around her without slackening pace. None the less, the impression persisted. She found herself walking more and more quickly; it required control not to break into a run.

You're imagining things, she told herself. You had a bad knock and you have exerted more today than at any time since the accident. The accident, she repeated firmly to herself.

She plunged recklessly down the dingy, dark steps of the subway, bought a token and went through the turnstile onto the platform with an odd sense of escape. A throng of high school students whooped and shouted on the center of the platform and she moved away to stand alone toward the end. Again she was aware of that irrational sense of fear and she drew nearer the noisy youngsters, the boys shoving and showing off for the benefit of the squealing girls. The platform vibrated as the train thundered out of the tunnel and rushed toward them.

The blow struck her between the shoulders and Kay pitched forward in front of the oncoming train. Something jerked her arm, her feet flailed wildly, and then she was on the platform, held in the strong grip of one of the boys. A white-faced boy.

"You shouldn't have done that," he managed to say.

"I didn't jump. Someone pushed me."

He didn't believe her, but he helped her onto the train, steered her toward an open space on the bench, and then backed away to join his now-silent friends. She sat huddled on the seat, terror still dominating her. She could feel the onrush of the train, its hot breath on her. To reassure herself she pressed her feet firmly on the floor. You are safe, she told herself. Safe. She looked up to see the oddly silent youngsters staring at her as though trying to find in her face some clue to the woman who had wanted to die.

With the automatic awareness of the New Yorker, she counted off stations, managed to get to her feet. For a moment she clung to the center pole to steady herself, then she squared her shoulders, lifted her head, smiled into the boy's accusing eyes.

"You saved my life, you know. I am very grateful."

Just the same, she thought, as she climbed subway stairs, emerged into the narrow, thronged canyon of lower Broadway, turned into the entrance of a towering office building, someone pushed me. Someone wanted me to die.

The receptionist looked at her in faint surprise as she took her name, and Kay caught her reflection in the glass of a painting on the wall, hat on the back of her head; eyes, as Mrs. Brundle had said, like black holes in a piece of dough. She straightened her hat and turned to face Malcolm Stoddard, who had come out to greet her.

"You've been overdoing it, Kay," he said after an appraising look. "Rushing things. You need more time to recuperate."

When he had pulled a comfortable chair forward for her in his big, sunlit corner office with a magnificent view of the bay, the Statue of Liberty shining in the sun, he said in concern, "You shouldn't have attempted to come to New York until you were quite well."

"I was all right when I left home this morning, but a quarter of an hour ago someone deliberately tried to kill me."

She saw the welcome die on his lips, the wariness return to his eyes.

When she had finished telling him, he said, "You are sure you didn't black out or have a dizzy spell?"

"No, and I had thought someone was following me ever since I left Ernest's apartment."

His eyes flickered. "Did any of the high school students see someone near you?"

"They were fooling around, shoving each other, showing off."

"Isn't it possible that one of them might have knocked against you unintentionally?"

She shook her head.

"But my dear child, why would anyone —"

"It must be the man who killed Ernest. He must know I saw him. There's no other possible motive. I think, Mr. Stoddard, you are going to have to accept my story as true." When he remained silent, she asked wryly, "Is there any part of it that you do believe?"

He was a deliberate man, not to be hurried, and she had just given him a considerable shock. She was aware that she must wait until he had digested it.

"Actually," he said at length, "I am prepared to believe a good deal of it. I've been looking into Paul Forbes's affairs. He was practically wiped out in the market five years ago. When I think of his consummate knavery in urging your father to take his business out of my hands and let him manage it —"

Kay surprised them both by laughing. "Uncle Paul a consummate knave! That's absurd, Mr. Stoddard. He was just trying to bolster up his faith in himself. He honestly thought he could protect Dad's interests."

"You're the same, Kay, always giving people the benefit of the doubt." For the first time his smile was genuine, then he sobered. "There's no doubt that Paul sold your father's stocks and no trace of any reinvestment."

"I told you where the money had gone."

"But even suppose, Kay, that the whole fantastic thing is true, that Paul was hoarding it. Red and white striped canvas bags! He might as well have used a circus calliope."

"I thought of that, of course, but we had had those canvas bags for years. He wouldn't spend money for anything else, even if it would be safer."

Stoddard's arms lifted and dropped. "Then will you tell me," he asked, "how anyone managed to spirit them away? That's the only road. There were no other cars on the road. The bags must have been garishly conspicuous as well as both bulky and heavy. If someone stole them, how did he get them away, unseen, before the troopers arrived? I've reported your story to them and they say categorically that it couldn't be done."

"But I put those bags in the Ford myself and they are gone," Kay reminded him, "so it was done. Regardless. And before I get through, I'm going to prove it."

Stoddard leaned forward to move a massive jade pen set, obviously never used, a fraction of an inch. "Perhaps," he said in a neutral tone, "you had better leave the whole thing in the hands of the authorities."

"I wish I could, but as they don't believe me, they aren't going to do anything, are they?" When Stoddard made no reply, she said, "Leav-

91

ing aside the important thing — what was done to Ernest — do you expect me to sit back and not even try to find the money?"

"In view of the — uh — deliberate attempt to injure you — providing it really happened — do you think you are wise to go ahead with this? I told you once before it's not healthy to know a murderer."

"When people once surrender to fear, they are defeated. I am not going to surrender, Mr. Stoddard."

"I admire your spirit, Kay, but I don't think much of your judgment in this case." He smiled into her stormy eyes and checked his remonstrance. "If you are right about this attempt on you in the subway, I am glad at least that you'll have a reliable man at hand in the studio. Have you met Ransom yet?"

"No, we passed on the road as I was leaving this morning."

"By the way, he paid three months rent in advance, so I have a nice check for you."

"Fine. And I arranged this morning to sell my cooperative apartment. No trouble at all because there was a waiting list. And that will be an even nicer check."

"I'm glad to hear it. You say you visited Billings's apartment?"

She nodded, and again her eyes were shadowed. "It seemed so terrible that he could just — go like that and no one know. But the owner tells me someone came in one night last week and removed all his belongings. I suppose it must have been the government people, though it seems like an odd way to do it."

"This man Billings is very elusive, Kay. Very elusive. I checked through a reliable, high-echelon source. No passport has ever been issued to Billings, so it's unlikely he was out of the country as he told you. And, whatever his job was, he was not working for the government."

CHAPTER 7

"The queer thing is that there is no record of his military service. In fact, there is no record at all of Ernest Billings."

"He must have been using that name as a cover for his work," Kay said at last. She added defensively, "I'm sure he would have told me, but we had so little time. We got engaged all of a sudden and it was too late that night to talk about things. The next day, what with that unseasonable blizzard and the situation at Uncle Paul's — and then when we were alone in the studio the man on snowshoes appeared. Ernest followed him to prevent him bothering Uncle Paul. After that we left the house in an awful rush. There just wasn't time to talk. You simply haven't been in touch with the right department."

"My friend in the government called me yesterday to say they had just made a thorough search of Billings's apartment."

"But how did they get in without Mrs. Willows's knowledge?"

"He didn't volunteer the information and I didn't ask. What interested the government boys was that Billings had lived in that apartment for three months and there wasn't a single fingerprint!"

"As though," Kay said, her mouth dry, "some-one is deliberately wiping out any trace of him." She told him then of the man who, a week after Ernest's death, had removed all his personal be-longings from the apartment.

Stoddard made a helpless gesture. "It's a very peculiar situation. Perhaps it's just as well —" Seeing her expression, he broke off sharply.

Kay looked at her watch. "I have a train to catch."

Stoddard picked up her sable cape and stood motionless, staring. She looked at him in sur-prise.

"See here!" At the sharpness in his tone she followed his eyes. There was a deep slash in the fur between the shoulders. "Turn around." She did so and heard him catch his breath. "Take off your jacket." The jacket of her suit, too, was cut. Under it she wore a jersey blouse with a zipper fastener in back.

"The knife caught on that zipper," Stoddard said, as though there was an obstruction in his throat. "That's what saved you. Oh, my God, Kay!"

"And now do you believe that Ernest was murdered?"

"This thing has got to stop," he declared in so pontifical a tone that she burst into laughter that was edged with hysteria. "You had better come home to Long Island with me tonight. My wife will be delighted."

Recalling Mrs. Stoddard, Kay thought this

highly improbable. "I want to go back to Connecticut. The house will be safe enough; it's locked up like a bank. And I'll have an able-bodied man in reach; two of them, in fact."

"If you are sure." He looked at her doubtfully. "Meanwhile, I'll see that this is reported to the proper authorities and try to have a check made on people cashing hundred dollar bills."

"So you believe me at last!"

He accompanied her to the elevator. "I don't like having you go up there alone," he admitted.

"I'll be all right."

Her confident tone reassured him. It was a pity, she thought, that it couldn't reassure her. She did not want to go back to Uncle Paul's house, but she had to go. Ernest's murderer had had no opportunity to escape with the canvas carry-alls. That meant that he must have taken the only possible direction and gone back up the hill to the house. Then the troopers had come and the doctor and the nurse with the watchdog. In those three weeks while Kay had been ill, there had been no opportunity to approach the house and retrieve the money. So he would come back and there was no one but Kay who could recognize him.

As the train slowed for her station, she began automatically to collect her things, smooth on gloves, slip the sable cape over her shoulders, the cape through which a knife had slashed. She wished now that she had been able to tell Malcolm Stoddard what she had in mind, but she knew he would not have allowed her to return, he would have had troopers guarding the house, preventing the return of the man with the long pointed upper lip. And Kay desired his return almost as much as she feared it. The man who had sent Ernest to his death — and the horror never left her that Ernest might still have been alive when the car burst into flames — was going to pay for it.

Feeling like an avenging fury, Kay stepped out on the platform and met the startled eyes of the local cab driver who was waiting for passengers. He climbed into his empty cab, raced the motor, and backed out of the parking lot.

Kay stared after him in dismay. How on earth was she going to get home? Then she was seized from behind and kissed exuberantly.

"Kay sweetie! We hoped you'd be on this train."

"Charlie Hammond! Sylvia! I thought you were in Italy."

With one of the Hammonds on either side, their arms around her, she was swept off the platform and into a big Chrysler.

"We can all sit in front," Sylvia declared. "You're so slim —"

"If she loses five more pounds, she'll slip down a crack. I like my women plump," Charlie said in disapproval.

"Like me." Sylvia sighed. "Sometimes I think he's just fattening me up for the kill."

"Whatever my intentions may be, my lips are

sealed," Charlie said darkly.

"That will be the day!" Sylvia put her hand on Kay's arm and her voice sobered. "We heard about the accident, of course, but I didn't realize until I saw you —"

"Tact, my love. Tact. If I had been in the diplomatic service, where my family wanted me to be, you'd have wrecked our foreign relations for fair. And speaking of relations," Charlie rattled on, "we are about to be besieged. A distant cousin is arriving tomorrow with three youngsters who are run down and need, and I quote, the peace and quiet of the country. So this being our one night of freedom, you'll have dinner with us, of course."

"I'd love to if you will ferry me. Uncle Paul's car —" Her voice wavered.

"Transportation goes with the dinner," Charlie assured her. "Positively no extra charge."

"We just came home this morning and we saw all kinds of activity going on at the studio," Sylvia said.

"I've rented it for three months to Deke Ransom."

"Deke Ransom! What gorgeous fun. That's a man I have always yearned to know. Is he as attractive as people say?"

"I haven't even met him yet, but he was interested in the studio and I was interested in the rent." Kay felt rather than saw the startled exchange of glances between husband and wife. Sooner or later she would have to explain the situation but for the moment she was content merely to be with them. The Hammonds were, she thought, the happiest couple she knew but, unlike most couples who have attained a really happy marriage, they did not exclude others.

"Would you like to stop at the house before you come up to our place?" Sylvia asked.

"Just to change. It won't take but a few minutes."

"If you ask me, all Sylvia wants is a look at her hero," Charlie declared, as he pulled up before the house and they all piled out of the car. "Scraping up an acquaintance with a celebrity; downright vulgar, that's what it is."

Kay started up the walk and stopped abruptly as she heard the deep bark of a boxer, which leaped toward her.

"Down!" At the man's sharp command the dog halted, turned back.

At the same time Sylvia cried out, "Kay, you've got a great rip in your sable cape; it's practically falling off you."

"Someone stabbed me this afternoon and tried to push me off a subway platform."

The Hammonds cried out and the man stopped short. He was slight of build, perhaps in his middle thirties, casually dressed in slacks and a turtle-neck sweater. His manner was casual too, the casualness of a person who is as self-confident as he is unself-conscious. He bent over to snap on the leash.

"I'm awfully sorry," he said. "Deacon won't

misbehave when he has been properly introduced. By the way, I am Deke Ransom."

"I am Kay Forbes. I hope you'll find the studio
comfortable, Mr. Ransom."

"It is charming, and everyone has been most
helpful. A Mrs. Brundle has already offered to
do the heavy cleaning. Very friendly." His eyes
brushed over Kay's face, moved on, half questioningly, to the Hammonds.

"Mr. and Mrs. Hammond, my nearest neighbors and dearest friends. Mr. Ransom, my tenant."

"And if you say, 'Not *the* Mr. Ransom,' I'll
strangle you, my love," Charlie declared as he
shook hands.

"I don't need to. I've seen his pictures. And
the reason I insisted on stopping here was because I hoped I'd meet him," Sylvia declared.

"It's a pity," Deke laughed, "that you can't
hear me purring. The amount of flattery I can
swallow is incredible." Charlie gave him a shrewd
glance and grinned.

"Kay," Sylvia said, her voice sober, "was that
true about someone trying to — to —"

"Kill me," Kay said steadily. "Yes, it was."

"Want me to go in with you while you
change?"

"No, I'm not nervous about the house."

"No one," Ransom assured her, "gets past
Deacon. And that reminds me, you had better
get acquainted now so there won't be any further
misunderstandings. Manners, Deacon!"

Gravely the big dog held out its paw, which Kay accepted. Then she let him sniff her hand.

"Friend," Ransom told him and Deacon sat down, regarding Kay, who patted him rather tentatively. "It will be all right now, Miss Forbes. And we always keep him on a leash unless he is having a run with one of us at hand. Don't be afraid of him."

"I won't," Kay said dubiously. "But when I come home tonight, will he —"

"Why," Sylvia said impulsively, "don't you dine with us tonight, Mr. Ransom? If we're going to be neighbors, let's start now. And then you could see that Kay gets in without the boxer bothering her."

Deke Ransom was somewhat taken aback, but after a half-questioning look at Charlie, who said, "Now that's a sound idea," as though he meant it, he accepted.

It wasn't until after Charlie had refilled their cocktail glasses and the four of them sat, relaxed and as much at ease as though they had known each other all their lives — an atmosphere the Hammonds managed, without effort, to generate around them — that Charlie said, "What was that about someone trying to hurt you today, Kay?" He had a round face, merry eyes, and normally babbled like a brook, but now his kindly face was sober as he studied her.

"Don't make her talk if she doesn't feel like it," Sylvia said quickly. She was a tall, angular girl with hair so pale a blonde that it was almost platinum and a narrow, high-cheekboned face that was vivid without being pretty.

"There's not much use," Kay said wearily. "No one believes me. They say there's a queer streak in the Forbeses. They say I imagine things. They — why, the local taxi driver is afraid of me; he wouldn't even take me to the train this morning and he practically ran when he saw me returning this evening. And everyone says I had a brain injury last year when — John died. Everyone says I'm crazy when I swear I never touched Ernest's car, that I saw someone kill him." Her voice began to shake treacherously. "Dr. Grantling wants to put me in Fenwick. But just the same someone is trying to wipe out every trace of Ernest, and today someone with a knife struck me and tried to push me under a subway train."

There was a long silence in the big rambling living room. Then Sylvia said, sounding very practical and matter of fact, "Well, I must say it's high time we came home. When I think of you going through all that by yourself — but you've got us now. And I can tell you one thing, they'll send you to Fenwick over my dead body."

Kay set down her glass because her hand was shaking too much to hold it.

"But, Kay," Charlie began, "why —"

Ransom intervened smoothly. "I think Miss Forbes has had about all she can take today."

After a quick look at his guest, Charlie said, "We always expect our guests to sing for their supper. Sylvia is panting to hear about some of your experiences."

Sylvia panted loudly.

"You sounded," Charlie said critically, "more like an engine getting up steam, but still it was a good effort."

All through dinner Deke, in response to Sylvia's prodding, discussed his travels, the people who had posed for him, while he interviewed them for the Talking Portraits which had become so famous.

"What's the hardest part," Charlie asked, "getting the interviews or getting the facts?"

"There's no trouble about getting interviews, not, at least, in the vast majority of cases," Deke said. His forehead furrowed as he thought. "The chief problem, of course, is detecting which ideas they are trying to put across, using me as a publicity machine. As far as facts are concerned —"

"What is truth, said jesting Pilate, and did not stay for an answer," Charlie commented.

"Oh, approximate truth, of course. Insights, perhaps. The person I can grapple to my heart with hooks of steel is the one who thinks for himself. More and more people are linking up with one or another ideology. There's so much simplification. It's easy to let Big Brother tell you what to think, and to me Big Brother wears a swastika as well as the hammer and sickle, and he's more indigenous to our soil, God help us. It's easy to respond to the hate cries, usually carefully wrapped up in a flag. Perhaps hate is the greatest simplifier of them all. It's the man with the throb in his voice, the man with the easy formula, the man who tries to shout to my emotions instead of speaking to my mind, the man who is sure he is right, that I run from like hell."

"You sound," Sylvia remarked, "rather fed-up."

"Not really. Even when the mess people get themselves into is maddening and frustrating, it is always interesting. Anyhow, one can't afford to throw in the towel."

"You're sort of a lone wolf in your field, aren't you?" Charlie commented when they had drifted into the music room for coffee. "I don't think I'd like that. I'm used to having my wench around. A poor thing," he added disparagingly, "but my own."

"My wife traveled with me for several seasons," Deke said, his voice colorless. "She died in Cairo three years ago." He nodded toward the piano. "It's your turn," he said with a grin.

"And don't," Charlie's adoring wife suggested, "pretend to be modest about it. You know you're dying to show off."

The room was lighted only by candles and a fire that blazed in the hearth. Charlie played softly, his stubby ugly artist's hands ranging from Scarlatti to Schubert and then a queer, difficult jangling thing of Prokofieff. Finally, he played some melodies from his opera, sketching out, as he did so, the plot and action.

All evening they carefully ignored Kay who sat relaxed and quiet, the nightmare world dissolved in peace and contentment and the sure knowledge of the loyalty and affections of the Hammonds. Whether they believed her or not — well, that could wait. It seemed at this moment there was no urgency.

When she yawned, widely and noisily, Sylvia laughed. "That's the kind of stimulation we provide for our friends," she explained to Ransom.

"It's the first happy time I've had," Kay said simply. "But I'd better get some sleep. Mrs. Brundle will be at the house before nine and that jeep would wake up the dead." She caught her breath and went on, "Tomorrow, I must go down and see poor Nelly. I feel guilty about neglecting her."

"Poor Nelly, my foot," Charlie said rudely. "I've told you before that you are always wrong about people, Kay. Nelly is a troublemaker from way back."

"Oh, Charlie —"

"Look, Baby, use the head; that's what it is for. How do you think the taxi driver heard you were — uh — a bit crazy? That's our Nelly's work. She's a gossip and a malicious gossip. She's poison. Mrs. Brundle is all right, but she carries everything back to Nelly and Nelly broadcasts. How do you think we knew what had happened to you, and that you were coming in on that train this afternoon? How do you think we knew you weren't apt to have any transportation?"

"Charlie," his wife warned him.

"Believe me, Kay," he continued earnestly, "Noisome Nelly is not to be trusted an inch. You watch your step, gal."

As they were saying good night, Sylvia called, "Kay, let's get together tomorrow. We've got to talk about what happened on the subway platform today."

They drove home slowly, Deke with his hands steady on the wheel, eyes straight ahead. It was only as they pulled up at the house that he said, "Let me go in with you in case you are nervous."

"I'll be all right."

"Sure?"

"Quite sure. Good night, Mr. Ransom."

"You weren't hurt this afternoon?"

She shook her head. "Not even scratched. Just scared stiff, that's all."

He opened the door for her. "There's nothing to be afraid of here, Miss Forbes. If anything bothers you, anything, at any time, call the studio and I'll come over."

When she laughed, he said soberly, "I mean that."

"You are very kind, but, after all, I can't saddle you with my problems. They don't concern you."

"Don't they?" he said oddly.

CHAPTER 8

Before going upstairs, Kay made a quick tour of the lower floor, resisting a temptation to leave all the lights burning. She would be getting like Mrs. Prescott if she didn't watch out, afraid of her own shadow.

The uncarpeted stairs creaked under her feet. In fact, the whole house seemed to creak and stir as though, at night, it came alive. But all old houses made strange noises, she reminded herself, and this one was very old. At least it was warm now. When the porch had been repaired and the house repainted, with a few hundred dollars spent on redecoration and new furniture, with the treacherous stairs remade, it could be restored to much of its old charm.

While she undressed and brushed her hair — how Ernest had loved her thick dark hair; no don't think of that — she planned to renovate the house, considering it in detail, room by room. But before she got into bed she saw the sable cape lying across a chair, slit almost from top to bottom, and the horror came back.

With an effort of will she made herself switch out the light and then she could no longer escape into planning to improve the house. She began to relive the day, from her hysterical outburst when Mrs. Brundle had started down the hill to the discovery that someone had removed all traces of Ernest from his apartment, wiping him out as his fingerprints had been wiped out, obliterating him.

"I won't let them do that to you, Ernest," she muttered and heard her own voice. Talking to oneself was a bad sign. She knew that. She pressed her fingers over her lips as though to silence herself.

"But I didn't imagine the knife that slit my coat," she said abruptly. "That was real. That happened."

Again she felt the tingling along her spine that she had experienced when she believed someone was following her. She felt the sudden shove, the moment of ghastly terror when she lost her balance and stumbled at the edge of the platform in front of the oncoming train, the violent tug that had dragged her back to safety.

She began to shiver and turned up the thermostat on the electric blanket. The band of pain tightened over her head and she lay motionless so as not to jar it. She wouldn't be able to endure those headaches much longer, but she didn't dare consult Dr. Grantling about them. There was always the threat of Fenwick.

Malcolm Stoddard hadn't believed her until he saw the cape with the slit in it. Even the Hammonds had let the subject drop almost without comment. And people don't act that way when someone has nearly been murdered; they ex-

108

claim, they ask questions. But the Hammonds had been silent.

The sudden deep bark of a dog made her start. That was Deke Ransom's boxer. Her thoughts switched to her new tenant. For once a celebrity lived up to the advance billing. He was interesting and amusing and attractive, though it was hard to analyze his attractions. Not especially good-looking, but you didn't think about his looks; you were interested in catching glimpses of his personality, of his mind. She could call him if she needed anything, if she was frightened. He was right next door in the studio.

"But how," she wondered aloud, "did he hear of the studio and know I would be willing to rent it?"

She tried to turn her head and then lay still as pain stabbed at her. She couldn't take the headaches much longer. They were driving her mad.

It was the crown of spikes on her head that caused the trouble. If she could just take it off, she would be all right. Impossible to drive with the thing on and she wanted to drive carefully. John's car was so new that the interior still smelled of varnish and leather. The trouble was that there was a veil hanging from the crown of spikes, a veil that made it difficult for her to see. Like fog.

She strained to see the two misty figures across the bridge. They were struggling and, somewhere out of sight, a dog barked. One of the men raised his arm and there was a cry. It was her own attempt to shout a warning that awakened her.

She was drenched with perspiration. She stared wide-eyed at the ceiling, determined not to fall asleep again, not to return to the nightmare in which she had almost seen the face of the murderer.

The dog barked furiously and through the window she could see lights flash on in the studio, could hear a low command. The dog growled and then was silent. There were fireflies on the lawn. No, they must be flashlights. Before the lights were finally turned off, Kay's heavy eyelids had dropped. This time she slept without dreaming.

The noisy arrival of Mrs. Brundle's jeep awakened her. The room was sunlit and her night fears remote, almost forgotten. Almost. She slipped into a robe and went downstairs to admit the housekeeper.

"Your uncle," Mrs. Brundle wheezed, "didn't put a chain on that back door after he took sick so's I could let myself in." She surveyed Kay disparagingly. "You look like something the cat dragged in," she commented. "You better go back to bed, Kay. I'll bring you a tray."

"All I need is some coffee. There's some instant if you don't want to bother."

Mrs. Brundle snorted. "I guess I've got strength enough to make real coffee."

Kay pulled herself up the stairs to dress. For the first time she saw herself in the mirror, skin dull and colorless, eyes sunken and shadowed.

She bathed and dressed bravely in a becoming red wool dress — Ernest had liked her in red; stop it and think of something else. With the help of make-up she looked less like a zombie, she decided.

Mrs. Brundle had provided an ample breakfast of fruit, hot cereal with heavy cream, and biscuits that were as light as a feather.

"Let me see you eat every scrap of that," she ordered. "You shouldn't of gone to New York so soon. You're all wore out."

Remembering Charlie Hammond's warning about Nelly, Kay did not mention the attempt to push her off the subway platform and she reminded herself to take her suit and fur cape to a tailor before the housekeeper discovered them. She had better take them to New York; she couldn't afford any more local gossip. No getting away from it, village people talked. She still remembered the woman who had been congratulated on having a new car just five minutes after leaving the bank where she had arranged to finance it.

The night had left her drained of energy. It wasn't rest she needed, it was fresh air and exercise. After breakfast she went up to her room, put the slashed garments out of sight, and got into a wool jacket, a scarf over her hair.

She came down in search of garden gloves. "Mrs. Brundle, who did the gardening for Uncle Paul? The autumn leaves weren't cleared off last fall and the place is a mess. If I'm going to put it on the market, it ought to be in better shape."

"Mr. Forbes didn't hire anyone last year. Did what he could himself. Tell you what," Mrs. Brundle added, as though the thought had just struck her, "I'll ask my lodger. He likes to get exercise and though he can't see good he might like the work. You know, give him a little cash and he might want to stay on permanent. Only thing is, he's not strong and he sleeps late in the morning. But he could help out after-noons."

"You might ask him to talk to me," Kay said absently, pulling on garden gloves.

From one of the living rooms where she was running a carpet sweeper — both rooms were open and warm now — Mrs. Brundle suggested, with a diffidence that was alien to her, "Well, it would be nicer if you did it yourself. Asked him, I mean. He'd appreciate it, and I wouldn't want him to think — that is, Nelly —" She broke of. Then she called sharply, "Come here, Kay!"

She was standing in the living room that had so long been unused. "Just take a look at that! Now I ask you!"

Kay's eyes traveled around the room, returned with a question to Mrs. Brundle. "I don't see anything wrong."

"Someone," Mrs. Brundle said, "has been searching this place. Look at that fire screen. I always fold it like this." She demonstrated. "And those big books on the bottom shelf of the book-case. Mr. Forbes kept them in a certain order.

Now they are every which way."

"But —"

"Someone got in here yesterday. I can tell. I was dusting just before I took you to the train in the morning. Everything was all right then."

"But —" Kay began again.

Mrs. Brundle, her heavy face highly flushed, went charging out of the room. In a moment she called triumphantly from the other living room, "In here, too." When Kay followed her, she pointed out, "That vase on top of the cabinet was always on the doily. Now it ain't. And you can see where the couch was moved. See those depressions on the carpet? No one had moved that couch in months. I know I should of," she added quickly, "on account of saving the carpet. But I only worked here three hours a day and did the cooking and all. And," her voice rose, "look at that!"

Kay followed the pointing finger to the long draperies at one of the windows. "See, I always keep them tacked down so they'll hang just right. Someone pulled out this tack to look behind them." She held it accusingly in her thick palm.

"Well," Kay said weakly.

"Mrs. Prescott kep' saying there was something wrong with this house," Mrs. Brundle went on, now well into her stride. "You can ask poor Nelly how often I told her about it. The way that dog went on at nights and all."

"So," Kay said, "does Mr. Ransom's dog. It barked last night until I nearly went mad."

"Look, Kay, no getting away from it, there's something wrong with this place. I wish you wouldn't stay here."

"I have to," Kay told her bluntly. "I can't afford to live anywhere else and I've moved out of my New York apartment."

"There's the Hammonds. Nelly heard they was back and they always set great store by you, Kay."

"I'll think about it." As she opened the back door, Kay added, "I hope no one hears about this. There's been enough gossip."

"Of course not," Mrs. Brundle said. "I won't say a word, and where people pick up these things, I can't imagine. You want to know what I think, it's these party lines on telephones are to blame. Snoopers with no business of their own to mind. Nelly says she can always tell when someone listens in. Once she could even hear a radio in the background. Course Nelly spends a lot of time on the telephone. Poor girl, she's mighty lonely, and so few visitors."

Hearing the reproach in her voice, Kay said guiltily, "I'll go down to see her this afternoon. I can walk it without trouble. And that reminds me, as long as I have no transportation, I'll leave you a shopping list every day."

It was a relief to escape from the house, even sunlit as it was this morning. The air, crisp and clear, filled her lungs and after kicking idly at autumn leaves for a few minutes, Kay went around to the shed back of the kitchen where she found a lawn rake. The leaves were matted and soggy and unexpectedly heavy. For a little while she worked, making small progress and hoping that she was not tearing up lawn as well as removing leaves.

Something stirred at her feet, seeming to touch her, and she whirled around in a rush of fear. The boxer panted amiably and lent his assistance, scattering the leaves she had drawn into a pile.

"I see you have a new helper, Miss Forbes." Deke Ransom had come across the lawn so quietly that she had not heard his approach. He stood easily, hands in his pockets, head a little on one side, smiling at her.

"Good morning."

Something in her expression, her hostile tone, made him raise his eyebrows. "Let me do that, won't you?" He took the rake from her hand and began drawing the leaves together with long, easy movements.

For a time it appeared that the silence between them was to remain unbroken. Then he tossed a stick to Deacon, who raced after it and returned to drop it hopefully at Kay's feet. She laughed and threw it for him. The boxer dashed off, strewing leaves.

"I'm afraid," Deke said, "he disturbed you last night. I've never known him to do that before."

"Yes, I heard him. You came out to look around, didn't you?"

"Both Max and I. Max is my houseman. There was a prowler, but no one gets past Deacon."

Again silence fell while Kay played with the boxer and Deke raked up leaves.

"I think," Kay said at last, "that someone must have got past Deacon. My house was searched while I was in New York yesterday. And I didn't," her voice began to rise, "imagine it."

He met the accusation in her eyes and took her by surprise. "Steady, Kay. Steady. I believe you. But don't — look like that. No one will get into your house again. That's a promise. Even if Max and I have to take turns sitting up with a shotgun."

For some reason, Kay found it hard to look away. When she had done so, she leaned over to pat the boxer, which had stretched out, panting at her feet. "But someone did get in," she said flatly. "And it happened after you arrived with Deacon. So it must have been your couple or —"

"Or me. Yes, I see. Awkward, isn't it? Why don't you pay a visit to the studio and look over the suspects for yourself?"

His lips showed only amusement but there was something challenging in his eyes that made her say crisply, "That's a good idea."

Even in one day the studio had taken on the personality of its new tenant. A fire crackled on the hearth. Half a dozen canvases were stacked against the wall. An easel had been set up where it got a north light. Tubes of oil paints had been tossed carelessly into an open metal box. Her Steuben bud vase held an assortment of brushes.

For the first time Ransom seemed to be aware of the disorder. "Sorry," he apologized. "Right now the place is a shambles, but we'll settle down in a day or two and get it in order. The problem is knowing what to do with those canvases."

"There's a storeroom back of the kitchen. I'm afraid it is filled with junk, but I'll weed it out so you'll have extra space."

"That will be fine."

"The only trouble is that there are rats in there."

Deke grinned. "We'll cope with the rats before you venture in. But we'd better not mention them to Wilma. My cook is," he paused, "rather high-strung and nervous."

"Remind me to give you the key to the storeroom," Kay said. "Uncle Paul kept everything locked up."

Deke looked down at her feet in concern. "Good Lord, you've been wading through those wet leaves without boots. Your shoes are soaked. You can't afford to do that sort of thing. Wilma!"

Kay found herself settled on the big couch facing the fire. Deke knelt before her to slip off her wet shoes and turn them on their sides so they could dry. Then, in spite of her protests, he took one slim stockinged foot in his hand and began to rub it vigorously.

"They're like ice. Wilma!"

The girl in maid's uniform who came out of the kitchen was very young, not more than twenty, with delicate features. She would have been pretty if it had not been for the curiously blank look in her large blue eyes. She moved like a sleepwalker, and then stood with one hand against the door frame as though she required a support.

"Did you call me?" Her voice was slow and dull.

"Miss Forbes is chilled. Will you make some coffee and bring a bottle of rum? That should warm her up. Oh, first bring a big bath towel. She got her feet wet."

The blank eyes turned from Kay to Deke on his knees, rubbing a cold foot between his warm hands. Even as Kay became aware of the extraordinary sensation, as she half attempted to withdraw the foot and his hands tightened on it, she saw the girl looking at her with a curious intentness, a naked hostility. Why, Kay thought in dismay, Mrs. Brundle was right. There's something wrong with that girl.

Then Wilma withdrew silently and Kay was conscious only of the hands that clasped her foot — of all the absurd — she felt color flooding her cheeks and she was helpless to prevent it — of all the ridiculous — she met Deke's demanding eyes and could not break away from them.

There were voices in the kitchen and Deke, breathing rather fast, was rubbing the other foot. A man in slacks and sweater came in with some logs, brushed past Deke to stack them in the metal log basket, and stood wiping his hands, inspecting Kay in a cool leisurely way. Watching eyes, Mrs. Brundle said. She had been right about that, too. Whatever preposterous current of emotion Deke had established between them, Kay was aware that she neither liked nor trusted his couple.

Max pulled a bath towel off his shoulder where he had slung it. "Wilma said you wanted this."

"Thanks, Max. Hurry up that coffee and rum, will you?"

"Wilma is working on it." The man's eyes left Kay's face, dropped to her stocking feet, moved on to Deke with sudden speculation. Then he went out.

Deke's lips compressed and he bit back whatever he wanted to say.

"Independent isn't he?" Kay remarked.

Deke shrugged. "Oh, I don't give the orders around here. I take them." He sounded rather bitter.

CHAPTER 9

Warmed by the coffee with its shot of rum, Kay found herself, relaxed and at ease, talking with Deke as though he were one of the Hammonds. Deacon lay at her feet as though he had accepted her right to be there. By some tacit agreement the subject of the search of her house had been dropped although Kay suspected that the enigmatic Max had had something to do with it and that Deke was aware that the search had been made.

While Deke talked, he pulled a notebook from his pocket and sketched idly. Then he crumpled up the sketch and tossed it in the general direction of the fireplace.

With a little exclamation Kay bent over to retrieve it, smooth it out. In a few strokes he had caught Deacon in the act of leaping for a stick. The sketch was a small miracle of action.

"Oh, don't throw it away!" she cried in protest. "It's so awfully good."

"You want it?" He was surprised. "I can't seem to think without a pencil in my hand."

"Oh, may I have it? Will you sign it for me?"

He laughed as he obeyed. "None genuine without this trademark. But that one's crumpled, no good. I'll do something else for you."

"That would be wonderful."

"It's unlucky, you know, to give a gift without a return."

She looked at him questioningly.

"I want you to promise me something, that you'll leave your house. You're not safe there. I didn't like that business last night. There was a prowler around the premises. Deacon doesn't act up unless something is wrong."

"Something is wrong. I've been saying that for three weeks but no one believes me. They think I imagine things."

"I'll believe you, Kay. That accident yesterday; you said someone tried to kill you in New York."

"You see I'm no safer away from the house than I am in it."

"Why?" he asked bluntly.

"Mr. Stoddard warned me that it isn't healthy to know a murderer."

"I suppose," he said at length, "you know what you are talking about."

She nodded. "And there's more to it. I won't rest until I've tracked down that murderer and exposed him. I won't stop until," and her voice was shaking again, "he can't do any more harm."

"Don't be a fool, Kay!" he said with unexpected violence. "Whatever you may believe, leave these things to the police. They know how to handle them. That's what they are there for."

"You have a talk with them," she suggested; "and see for yourself just how far I'd get. There's not one person at the barracks who believes me.

They think I'm a mental case. They think I imagined what happened. Anyhow, even if they should believe me, they'd spoil things."

"Spoil them how?" He was quiet and relaxed again, only his eyes vividly alive.

"Stake out this house. Watch it. Scare him away."

"And you want the murderer to come back?"

"It's not just vengeance, an eye for an eye; it's not even the money, though God knows how much I need it. But he wasn't satisfied with killing Ernest; he wants to destroy every single trace of him."

"Were you so deeply in love with this man Billings?"

"I don't know," Kay said honestly. "I'm not sure. He was awfully attractive and — oh, gay of spirit. And confident. He made me feel safe."

Deke looked at her quickly, looked back at the sketch he was making in the small notebook. "It hardly sounds like the basis for a sound marriage."

"And he loved me."

"That," Deke commented, his eyes on the sketch, "wouldn't be difficult."

"I suppose I should have warned him." The headache was beginning to throb again. "I ought to wear a bell like a leper in the Middle Ages. I ought to carry a sign like that line of Donne's, 'Take heed of loving me.' It's happened twice, you know. Men fell in love with me and then they died."

"You're talking like a little idiot." Deke's tone was detached, but Kay felt as though a glass of cold water had been flung in her face. "Self-torture. Good God, isn't there enough real trouble in the world without conjuring up these phantoms, without developing a senseless feeling of guilt?"

"You don't understand."

Deke's pencil moved quickly and surely. "Don't I? Three years ago my wife died of food poisoning because she had gone to Cairo with me. She didn't like the place; she went because we," he hesitated, went on flatly, without emphasis, "liked sharing things. Without her they lost half their interest and ninety per cent of their excitement. So she died. If she had stayed home, she'd be alive today. I spent months of bitter remorse and self-recrimination. But people can't live like that. Flagellants are not really particularly nice or intelligent people, Kay." Unexpectedly he smiled at her. "Even when they are you and me."

He ripped out the sketch and handed it to her. For a long time she stared at the girl on the couch, heavy dark hair swept back from a good forehead. The warm passionate mouth at odds with the uncertain eyes that were looking, a startled question in them, into the eyes of the man on his knees before her. Only an arm of the couch and an edge of the table behind it had been drawn. On the table was the Steuben bud vase filled with brushes.

After an eternity Kay said brightly, "I see you unearthed that vase. Heaven knows where it has been all this time. We hadn't used it in years. In fact, the studio has been deserted for years."

He was smiling broadly.

To cover her confusion she asked, "By the way, how did you know about the studio? I hadn't advertised it."

The smile faded. He bent to examine her shoes, to restore them to her. "I learned about the place through my brother and I thought it might work out very well. I never guessed how well."

As she slipped on her dry shoes, he asked, "What really happened yesterday when you thought someone tried to kill you?"

"When someone did try to kill me."

She told him about her feeling that someone had followed her from Ernest's apartment. No, she hadn't been able to pick out any particular person among the crowds on the street who seemed interested in her. It was the kind of feeling she had when someone was staring at her. She had walked away from the noisy teen-agers on the subway platform and then, uneasy again, had drawn closer to them. The train was coming out of the tunnel but it hadn't begun to slow down when she had felt the blow between her shoulder blades and had plunged forward, pitching toward the tracks.

She had lost her footing, she was falling when the highschool boy caught her, hauled her back to safety. He had thought she was trying to kill herself. It wasn't until Mr. Stoddard had seen the slit in her fur jacket and in her suit coat that she had known about the knife. It had caught on a zipper on her blouse.

"God!" he whispered. At length he said, "Why do you think it happened?"

"Because I said Ernest had been murdered and I could identify the murderer. There's no other possible reason. It wasn't just an attempt to scare me. It was an attempt to — eliminate me, as Ernest had been eliminated. And if I had died under that train, the killer would have been safe. The cuts in my clothes wouldn't have shown up after the train had got through with me. People would have said suicide while of unsound mind. Even the schoolboy thought I had deliberately tried to throw myself under the train. And you can ask Dr. Grantling; he thinks there is something wrong with me."

She laughed suddenly. "Mr. Stoddard knows it really happened. He said," her laughter rose, "he said it's got to stop."

"Yes," Deke said, "it's got to stop." His face was somber and his mouth looked tired beyond endurance.

He filled a pipe, taking his time; now that his disconcerting eyes were hidden, she was able to study his face and to observe that his forehead was more deeply lined than one would expect of a man in his middle thirties. It was a brooding, thoughtful face. As his breeding and cultivation

125

were revealed by his unstressed manners and his speech, so the stresses of his experience showed in the furrowed brow, the wry amusement of his mouth, the carriage of his head. A man who had a sense of personal involvement, not a man to be shoved around. If it weren't for his eyes — but he had lighted the pipe now and looked at her again. She bent hastily to adjust a shoe which had been perfectly comfortable before.

"That was an odd word you used. Eliminated."

"But that is what has happened to Ernest." She told him then about her visit to Ernest's apartment, from which all his personal effects had been removed, from which someone had wiped away every single fingerprint.

"At first I thought it must be a colleague of his. I had guessed from something he said that he was an undercover man in some government job. But Mr. Stoddard tells me that there is no government department with an Ernest Billings on its staff, so that may not even be his real name. And now I don't know how to trace him. He's just been — wiped out."

"Do you think he was the kind of man to have enemies?"

She shook her head.

"And yet you saw someone kill him in cold blood." There was a curious expression on his face.

"But that wasn't personal enmity. That was for Uncle Paul's money. I guess I had better explain. It's a long story. Am I boring you?"

He laughed joyously. "My dear!"

Kay began with Paul Forbes's letter, his appeal for — well, protection had been the word. She and Ernest had decided, just that very night, to marry and he insisted on going up with her.

"Did he realize what he was running into?"

"I didn't know myself until I saw the man outside the studio taking down Ernest's license number. Ernest went after him to find out what it was all about. So then Uncle Paul had to explain to me." Repeating the story of Paul's loss of his money through bad judgment, his conversion of his brother's stocks into currency, his hoarding, it sounded so fantastic that Kay wondered whether Deke would believe her. But he simply nodded for her to go on. He did not seem in the least surprised. He listened intently, checking off each point.

"So then I persuaded Uncle Paul to go back to New York with me. We would take the money with us, and I planned to put it in the bank next day, though Ernest thought we should let Uncle Paul have his own way with it as he couldn't live very long, and the shock of having it taken away might be more than he could endure. Then Uncle Paul refused to ride with Ernest because the man knew his car.

"Ernest was to go ahead, draw him off if he was still hanging around, and clear the way so I could drive Uncle Paul to New York in his old Ford, with the bags of money in the back of the car, covered by a blanket."

Deke moved to sit beside her on the couch. He took one of her tightly clenched hands and gently opened the fingers, flexed them.

"You see, I killed a man once. I was going to marry him but I drove his car, we hit a patch of fog, and John died. So I was afraid to drive. Petrified. And the hill was icy and there were no brakes on the Ford."

"Why weren't there?"

The question surprised her, broke her tension.

"Why I don't know. The car was old, of course, and —"

"Any brake trouble before?"

"Mrs. Brundle says everything was all right a few weeks ago when Uncle Paul last drove." Her eyes widened. "You mean that the brakes were fixed, that the man meant to kill us both?"

"It's a possibility, Kay."

"You're just trying to make me feel that I'm not responsible."

He knocked out his pipe. "Of course you aren't responsible. You're intelligent enough to see that. For some reason you don't want to see it. You're tormenting yourself and that's a stupid thing to do." He smiled at her. "Tell me exactly the way you remember the accident, not the way you have dreamed of it since."

"How do you know that?" She was startled.

"I've had bad dreams, too, and bouts of self-flagellation. Now about that accident."

For the first time in discussing it, even in remembering it, she was relaxed. She told him how the car had shot down the hill out of control, how Uncle Paul had screamed in terror, how the Ford had come to rest with the front wheels over the railing. She had blacked out then.

"But you do see, don't you, that I couldn't possibly have crashed into Ernest's car. I wasn't near it."

"What is the last thing you remember about the position of that Cadillac?"

"The man stopped Ernest at the foot of the ravine just as his car was turning onto the side road. Ernest got out and at first they just talked, then they were fighting. Then Ernest gave a kind of startled cry and fell."

"How was the visibility?"

"Poor. It was twilight and snow was falling and I couldn't risk taking a hand off the wheel to turn on the windshield wipers."

She glanced at her watch. "Good heavens, I've been here all morning! Mrs. Brundle will be furious if I let her lunch get cold."

He held her coat for her and stood for a moment with his hands resting lightly on her shoulders, as Ernest had stood in her apartment three weeks ago. He was aware of her rigidity, her resistance, and dropped his hands at once.

"Look here, Kay, you are sticking your head in a trap because you believe that money has been cached up here and you are waiting to snare a murderer."

"Well?" She sounded rather defiant.

"Has it occurred to you that you are remarkably trusting? How do you know I won't find the loot first and make off with it? I'm a complete stranger to you."

"But everyone knows who you are." She sounded bewildered. "You are a famous man. The very idea is ridiculous."

"You don't know much about people, do you?" For a moment she thought there was a kind of pity in his face, but she must be mistaken. There was no reason why he should be sorry for her.

"Why don't you go to the Hammond's?" he suggested. "They are good friends. You'd be only a quarter of a mile away if anything happened. I'll watch the place for you." He grinned without amusement. "As long as you are so trusting."

The telephone rang and he picked it up. He looked surprised. "Yes, she's here." He held out the phone to Kay.

Sylvia Hammond said, "Mrs. Brundle said I'd find you at the studio." She giggled. "A nice tidbit for Noisome Nelly to pass on. Ransom's not one to waste time, is he? Charlie saw it coming last night."

"Saw what?" Kay asked.

"I believe the French for it is *coup de foudre*. Conflagration. Chemical reaction. Whatever."

Kay laughed. "Don't be absurd."

Sylvia's mocking tone changed. "Darling, I'm so frustrated I could scream."

"What's wrong?"

"Charlie's cousins — removed to about the

hundredth degree but still family — arrived this morning. And guess what. One of the kids has chicken pox. What are we going to do?"

"He's not seriously ill, is he?"

"That's not the point. The thing is that Charlie and I wanted to bring you up here. We were horribly upset about that New York business, only we didn't speak of it last night. You looked as though you had just about had it and we wanted you to rest. But something has got to be done. We're worried sick about you."

"I'm all right," Kay assured her. "I'll be perfectly all right."

"But we haven't talked," Sylvia wailed, "not about anything that mattered, not about your —"

"Accident?" Kay said steadily. "And Ernest? Well, I'll be here until Uncle Paul's estate is settled, probably for months. There will be plenty of time to talk later."

"I don't like you being alone there," Sylvia said uneasily. "Neither does Charlie. It's all I can do to prevent him from knight-errantry of some idiotic sort. He'd probably end by giving you chicken pox."

Kay laughed.

"At least you have Deke Ransom within call."

"There's that, of course," Kay managed to sound detached.

"Kay, you don't sound like yourself. Oh, damn all distant cousins with chicken pox!"

CHAPTER 10

When Kay returned to the house, she found Mrs. Brundle seated at the wheel of the jeep.

"I thought you'd gone by now."

"Well, look, Kay." For once Mrs. Brundle was embarrassed, at a loss for words. "I was waiting for you. You've been eating alone too much and so, instead of cooking your dinner up here, I thought maybe you'd come down and have it with us. Be good for you to have a change."

The heavy red face wore a curiously wistful expression. Poor Nelly, Kay thought. Mrs. Brundle is hell-bent on keeping her new lodger for Nelly's sake and she wants me to give him a job. She was on the verge of refusing and then felt guilty. She had neglected Nelly for a long time. Oh, well, she decided, the lodger will have to look after himself.

"Fine! I'd enjoy that, and I haven't seen Nelly for months, not since last summer."

Mrs. Brundle beamed. "She'll be that pleased! And I've got a nice roast of beef and a lemon pie. No one, if I do say so, can better my lemon pie."

Kay's sympathy for the lodger ebbed. He might need qualities of self-preservation, but at least he was eating such food as he'd be unlikely to encounter again. She found herself wondering how many of Mrs. Brundle's ex-lodgers had, in later years, balanced her cooking against Nelly and wondered if they had not made a mistake.

This frivolous rumination so occupied her mind that the jeep had safely negotiated the hill and the bridge over the ravine before she was aware of it. Why, I wasn't even afraid, she realized, with a lift of the heart. She had made the trip not only without fear but without haunting memories.

"I see you was visiting Mr. Ransom this morning," Mrs. Brundle commented. "Nelly tells me he's real famous."

"He seems to be very pleasant."

"Nelly looked him up at the library. Last year he won two big awards: one for something like penetrating analysis in journalism, and the other for his pictures. Did you know he sometimes sells to collectors? Winston Churchill had a Ransom picture in his collection And there was something about his income. One of the highest-paid men in his field, it said. Nelly couldn't help wondering what he was doing here. When he travels abroad, he's entertained by dukes and everything. And yet he was right plain-speaking when I asked him about the cleaning. You'd never guess he was important by the way he acts."

Mrs. Brundle's cottage was in the village but not of it, on a narrow lane which contained several summer cottages. It was, Kay had always thought, the least inviting house she knew, so devastatingly clean and polished that one was afraid to step on the floor or sit in a chair for fear of leaving a footprint or mussing a cushion. A small Cape Cod, with a neat living room that was rarely used except when there were lodgers. A forbidding room. The floor was so highly waxed that the small rag rugs tended to skid under one's feet. Artificial flowers were arranged under a glass dome. There were doilies on chair arms and backs. Horsehair couch and chairs, both scratchy and precarious, were lined up rigidly against the wall.

Mrs. Brundle ushered her guest in with an air of triumph. Like bringing home a trophy, Kay thought in amusement. Nelly was sitting in the only rocking chair, a chair with an incurable creak, reading aloud from the *New York Daily News*. Across from her, lying back on the couch, his eyes hidden behind dark glasses, the new lodger, as Kay guessed by his heavy breathing, was asleep.

Nelly had changed in recent months. She must be nearly thirty. Up to now so thin as to appear scrawny, she had seemed like a child. Today, without appearing to have gained weight, she had a puffy look about her face, which was the color of wet clay, but to which she had added, without much judgment, a lavish use of make-up. Imperceptibly her youth had faded and she was a nondescript middle age.

Her brown hair was so thin that the scalp

showed through. Brushed up in a kind of pompadour, this had not been noticeable, but a cheap permanent wave had left her with vast areas of scalp like wayward paths across her head.

She broke off her reading and exclaimed in the little-girl voice that was so annoying, "Kay! I declare this is an unexpected honor. I never dared hope you'd take time for poor me, with your rich friends and all. Who could blame you?"

She fluttered her eyes. "May I present our lodger, Mr. Worth? Miss Forbes." She flashed a look of intimate understanding at the lodger.

The latter awakened, as Kay suspected, by their voices, stood up, peering in her general direction. His extreme pallor made her wonder how he could possibly undergo a serious operation. It was difficult to determine his age. He was quite bald and what hair he had was a rough, dry brown.

He smiled, revealing yellowed teeth. "How do you do?" His voice was repressed and he spoke slowly because of a speech impediment. "Won't you," he made a small uncertain gesture with his hand, "sit down?"

"She's come to have dinner with us," Mrs. Brundle said. "I told her I'd baked one of my lemon pies."

"I wondered why you would come here, of course," Nelly said with a little giggle that was tinged with malice.

"I'll just see about serving," Mrs. Brundle was

brisk. "Did you put the potatoes on, Nelly?"

Nelly sighed. "I do all I can. You know that, Ma."

"Of course you do, my brave girl. Kay, you can ask Mr. Worth if he's ever seen a better daughter."

"I've never seen one like her," Worth said, and Kay smothered a laugh. Poor Mrs. Brundle! Even the lemon pie would not weigh the scales against Nelly.

Mrs. Brundle hovered in the doorway. "Mr. Worth knows how Nelly is. Reads to him by the hour. And after that cataract operation he'll need just lots of sympathetic care."

"I seem to have come to the right place," Worth said politely.

Mrs. Brundle winked at Kay and nodded toward her lodger, apparently under the impression that, because of the dark glasses, he was completely blind to this by-play.

"All he needs," she said, staring significantly at Kay, "is to get out more, get some exercise, fresh air and all that to build him up."

Nelly slumped in her chair, emphasizing the thickening of her body, exclaimed petulantly, "I hate exercise! I don't see the sense in it. Mr. Worth ought to rest as much as he can."

Over to you, pal, Kay thought in amusement.

Mrs. Brundle gave Kay a last admonishing look and bustled out to the kitchen. She opened the oven and the little house was filled with the appetizing smell of roasting meat.

There was a small silence in the living room. Nelly put down the newspaper with a petulant gesture and went to set the table in the adjoining dining room, going reluctantly, as though unwilling to leave Kay and the lodger together. The latter, now that Kay was seated, had dropped back on the couch. She wondered whether he had fallen asleep again.

Nelly, distributing silver and napkins in the dining room, said protectively, "Mr. Worth don't talk much because he's got that impediment in his speech." Even for Nelly there should have been limits to tactlessness, but she went on, "And I don't see why he feels that way. It's different and kind of cute."

Seeing the man wince, Kay broke in hastily. "I'm here under false pretenses, Mr. Worth." She had his attention now, though she couldn't see his eyes. "Mrs. Brundle thought, as long as you have a lot of time on your hands, you might be persuaded to help me with the grounds up at the house. I warn you, the place has been neglected and there's a lot to do. But there is no one available in the village. I don't know whether you'd consider it; you could choose your own hours, of course. Anything you could do would be a godsend."

Nelly dropped a knife with a clatter. "You can see Mr. Worth is a sick man," she said sharply. "He needs lots of rest. He shouldn't overtax himself."

"I get plenty of rest," the lodger said in his

hesitant voice. "Never out of bed much before noon."

"But —" Nelly began.

"And, frankly, Miss Forbes, it would be a godsend to me, too. I need to be out of doors, to get some exercise, and I can't earn money any other way until after the operation. So if you'll really take me on, I'll do my best."

Nelly flounced into the kitchen where she could be heard whispering sibilantly to her mother. Kay impulsively held out her hand, realized the lodger had not observed the gesture.

"Wonderful! You've taken a load off my mind."

"That's mutual." The man had brightened perceptibly. He was taking care to control his stammer as though it might jeopardize the job. "When do I start and exactly what do you want done?"

"Why don't you walk home with me this afternoon so that you can look it over for yourself? But I warn you, the place is a shambles."

He smiled, revealing his discolored teeth. "I like a challenge."

"So does Kay," Nelly said. "I hear you've got Deke Ransom renting the studio. I've kept every article he ever wrote, Talking Portraits he calls them, with the pictures he drew of the people he interviewed, and all. He must of met just about every famous person in the world. Do you think you could get me his autograph?"

"Why, I don't know. I have no idea how he

feels about it. At least I could ask."

"I thought maybe you could," Nelly said spitefully. "Ma says you were over there first thing this morning." When Kay made no comment, Nelly went on, "Well, of course, it's at least three weeks since that man you were engaged to was killed, isn't it?"

The lodger broke into the conversation with stammering haste and, after a look from his shocked face to Kay's set one, Nelly fell uneasily silent and withdrew to the kitchen.

The meal, as lavish as though Mrs. Brundle had planned to feed a regiment, was as delectable as ever. When she had served large slices of lemon pie and coffee, she beamed at them.

"Everyone seems to like my lemon pie. My last lodger couldn't get enough of it. Once he ate three pieces at a single meal and came out at bedtime to see if there was any more."

"What would make a man leave a house where he could get cooking like this?" Worth wondered aloud.

"That," Mrs. Brundle admitted, "is what I'd like to know. He just upped and left without notice. Went out the day you had your accident, Kay, and he never come back."

"I hope he didn't owe you any rent."

"That's another funny thing. He'd just paid another week in advance that very morning."

"And he went without telling you?" Worth asked in surprise.

"More than that. He left behind all his clothes

and his suitcase and his equipment."

"Equipment?" Worth asked.

"He's a professional photographer. Can't say I was so much surprised at his going, just at the way he done it. Footloose fellows, say what you will. Out taking pictures of picturesque Connecticut. Fellows like that don't seem to take to the idea of settling down, and that's a fact."

"He was kind of cute, though," Nelly said. "But not — well, sociable, if you know what I mean."

Worth looked as though he knew what she meant and had a fellow feeling for the ex-lodger.

"What I mean is that, well, like I offered to learn how to develop films; things like that, you know, so I could help him."

"Nelly," her proud and hopeful mother declared, "always wants to help my lodgers."

Worth choked suddenly and Kay, to distract attention from his merriment, demanded, "But didn't you report that your lodger was missing?"

"Well, I figured maybe he'd just taken off to some new place." For a moment Mrs. Brundle's eyes rested anxiously on Nelly. "None of my business where he went, after all. He was free to do as he pleased. Anyhow, if they want to go, they want to go. No stopping them."

"What did you do with his things? Photographic equipment is apt to be very costly, particularly if he is a professional. He'd need all sorts of special gadgets."

"Everything is put away in the attic and safe

enough. He can have them whenever he wants them."

"It's very odd, isn't it? Do you suppose he was — oh, running away from something?"

Mrs. Brundle snorted. "Just like the stories you used to make up when you were a little girl. Come back one day to say a bear had chased you through the woods."

Kay laughed. "I'd just got that red cape for my birthday and I was pretending to be Little Red Ridinghood. It all seemed so real."

"You don't change a bit, Kay."

"No," Nelly said spitefully, "she doesn't. People in town are doing a lot of talking about that story you told of missing bags of money and someone murdering your fiancé."

I am not going to quarrel with Nelly, Kay told herself. She turned to Mrs. Brundle. "At least you haven't imagined your lodger's disappearance. You know it really happened."

"Look," Mrs. Brundle was worried, "do you think I ought to do something about it?"

"Yes, I do."

"The police, you mean?" Mrs. Brundle was visibly upset.

"Unless there is something in his belongings to tell you who he is, to provide some sort of address. If there is, you could inquire there first."

"There isn't a thing," Nelly said. "When we were putting away his stuff to clear the room for a new lodger, I went through it carefully, all the pockets and everything. Even the tags of where he'd bought his clothes had been cut out. And there wasn't a letter or a scrap of paper anywhere."

"What happened to the pictures he took?" Kay asked.

"That's what I'd like to know."

"The case of the vanishing lodger," Worth commented. "So you didn't really know a thing about the man."

"His name was Percy Willis," Nelly said. "I never knew anyone called Percy before. He was just my age. Twenty-six." She looked challengingly at Kay, who made no comment. "Nice manners and a nice way of talking, though he never said much. He'd just eat and go off somewheres. Never told me where he was going. Not so good-looking, but not homely, except he had a funny kind of mouth, a long upper lip that was pointed in the middle."

Kay's coffee cup rattled as she put it back on the saucer. "I'll have to get home," she said in a choked voice. "Thanks so much for a delicious meal, Mrs. Brundle."

"You don't look good," Mrs. Brundle said. "Maybe you'd better just set for a while. I'd drive you back, but I've got to get down to the drugstore to get Nelly's prescription filled."

"I'll walk back with her," Worth suggested. "I'd like to get a look at your place, Miss Forbes, and see what needs to be done."

The expression with which Nelly followed them to the door was venomous. Queer, Kay thought as she trudged back through the village, the lodger silent beside her, that she had never before been aware of Nelly's corroding jealousy. She had accepted her as poor Nelly, helpless victim of her infirmities. It had taken Charlie Hammond's warning to make her see for herself that in Nelly Brundle she had an enemy.

They walked slowly because Kay had automatically adjusted her pace to Worth's. She wondered in some concern whether she had been right in suggesting that he do the gardening. He seemed much too frail to handle it. She had let Mrs. Brundle maneuver her again.

At the ravine she halted instinctively, staring at the splintered railing, looking down at the spot where Ernest's car must have burned out. Both cars had, of course, been hauled away. There was nothing left but charred ground.

"Is this where it happened?" Worth asked, speaking carefully so that he could make himself understood. Seeing her face, he added apologetically, "Sorry, I shouldn't have mentioned it, but there's been so much talk. Nelly, of course, had all the details. And then some."

She turned to look back to where the side road turned off. That was where the Cadillac had stood, where the two men had struggled in the fading light, their figures blurred by the snow. Then she started up the hill, Worth silent beside her.

At the crest of the hill she spoke for the first time. "There you are."

"It's quite an estate."

"Oh I wouldn't expect you to look after the whole thing! Just the grounds around the house. I want the place tidied up because I'm putting it on the market."

Around the corner of the house Max strolled with Deacon leading the way. The dog growled and Max spoke to him sharply. Then he summed up Worth in a long, leisurely look that made Kay tingle with anger. What right had he to inspect anyone she chose to bring to the house?

Worth had stopped short. "My God, is that man-eater yours?"

"No, he belongs to Mr. Ransom." Seeing the man's hesitation, she added, "If you decide to work here, I'll make arrangements with Mr. Ransom to keep the dog out of the way when you come. You look around and see what you think. You can tell Mrs. Brundle whether or not you want to tackle it."

With a nod she went forward to meet Max. The boxer presented a paw which she shook gravely.

"I was just walking Deacon," Max said.

"Or patrolling?"

His expression did not change. "Well, there's that, too, of course."

"Where is Mr. Ransom? I want to see him."

"What's happened?" Max demanded sharply, saw her look of surprise and said awkwardly, "Sorry, I spoke out of turn but I thought something was wrong. He's working in the studio."

Frowning, Kay went to the studio. Through the big window she saw Deke standing before the easel. She tapped on the glass and went to the door where he was waiting for her.

"Come in." He asked quickly, "What's happened?"

She found herself laughing. "That's just what Max asked."

"Well, you look terribly excited."

"I am. Deke," she took a long breath, "I know who he is."

His face was blank. "Who is?"

"The man who killed Ernest."

"The hell you do!"

CHAPTER 11

"His name, or at least the one he's been using, is Percy Willis; he was masquerading as a photographer, and he was a lodger at Mrs. Brundle's. He disappeared without warning the day Ernest was killed, leaving everything behind him — his clothes and his photographic equipment. And he had just paid a week's rent in advance."

"How do you know it was the same man? Here," Deke added almost absently, "sit down. You must have come up that hill too fast. You're out of breath."

"Of course I'm out of breath. I was terribly excited. I could hardly wait —" She broke off.

He was quiet until she had settled in a big chair and accepted the cigarette he offered her. "Now tell me about it."

It seemed quite natural to do as he told her. She poured out the story of the lodger who had disappeared without warning and had left his belongings behind. Deke listened expressionlessly. When she finally came to the end, he merely nodded.

Max strolled in with Deacon, who came to flop comfortably at Kay's feet. She leaned over to pat him.

"The guy says to tell you he'll start right now,

146

if that's okay with you, Miss Forbes. Two dollars an hour, which is below the going rate."

"Fine," Kay agreed.

"I'll tell him it's all set then." Max looked from Kay to Deke, looked at the canvas on which Deke had been working, raised his eyebrows, and went out.

"Who's that?" Deke asked.

Kay had started to explain about her new gardener when her eyes fell on the canvas. So far the head had been only roughly sketched in, but Kay recognized it. Like Cleopatra, Mrs. Brundle had said.

"But I'm not like that," she protested.

He looked from her to the canvas. "Not yet," he agreed, "but the ingredients are there. They simply need to be — released."

Kay was too wise to ask questions, which seemed to amuse Deke.

"There's too much fear in the carriage of your head, too much guilt in your eyes. What are you afraid of, Kay, except perhaps — this?" With the handle of a brush he touched lightly the full, passionate mouth.

"I hurt people. I don't mean to, but I hurt them. My mother died when I was born. My closest friend in school caught a bad cold from me and got pneumonia and died. I killed Uncle Paul and John. I brought Ernest up here. Wouldn't you feel guilty?"

"That's a revolting display of self-pity if I ever heard one. If you think I'm going to give you the slightest scrap of sympathy, you are feeble-minded."

Kay sprang out of her chair. "You are the most arrogant, impertinent, impossible . . . Let me go! . . . Let . . . Deke, please . . . Deke, darling . . ."

"There's paint on your cheek," Deke remarked. "A streak of red that makes you look like an Indian preparing for battle."

"If you will practically assault a woman when you've got a paintbrush in your hand, what can you expect? And I feel more like an Indian after the battle." She was trying to restore order to her tumbled hair.

"Victorious?"

"I don't know. And what got into you? Of all the insane —"

He cupped her face in his hands. "Don't you know?"

"Well, I —"

He held her so she could not turn her head. "Kay?"

Her hands reached up to cover his. "Not now, Deke. Please, not now."

He let her draw away his hands without protest. "Of course."

Something made her turn her head sharply and she saw Wilma standing in the kitchen doorway. The blue eyes were not blank now, they were dark with hostility. She went running up the stairs and a door slammed.

Kay wondered how long the girl had been watching them. "What's wrong with that couple of yours? I wish you'd get rid of them."

"Sorry. I can't do that."

"Why on earth not?"

Deke changed the subject abruptly. "We got side-tracked. Tell me again about the missing lodger, Kay."

When she had repeated the whole story, he said, "And you are sure that was the same man who had been frightening your uncle?"

"And the same one who killed Ernest, and the same one who tried to kill Uncle Paul and me by tampering with the brakes. Yes, I'm sure. There was the long pointed upper lip. It's carrying coincidence too far to think there are two such men in a village of five hundred people, both of whom disappear on the same day."

"You may be right."

Deke did not try to keep her when she said she must get back to the house, but he strolled across the lawn with her, Deacon at his heels. Worth, busily raking up leaves, turned to smile, revealing his unsightly teeth. He was bareheaded and his bald head looked cold.

"That your new gardener?" Deke asked when they were out of earshot. "Doesn't look to me as though he could stay the course."

Kay explained about Mrs. Brundle conniving with her to supply the lodger with work so he could afford to stay on, hoping he would become attracted to poor Nelly.

Deke shook his head in disparagement. "It is borne in on me, more and more, that women have no ethical sense." He left her almost abruptly, running across the lawn to the studio, Deacon racing beside him. Kay heard him shout, "Max! Max!"

When she had locked, bolted, and chained the front door, Kay stood leaning against it. Her thoughts were in a turmoil of confusion. She had not known the man twenty-four hours and yet she — the memory of her uninhibited response to his kisses staggered her. As though there had been another self whose very existence she had not suspected, the one that only her mouth had betrayed.

What startled her most was that she felt only a deep exultation. You're a shameless wench, she told herself severely, and found that she was smiling. Then the smile faded and she felt the band tightening around her head. She had almost forgotten the headaches. She had found her first clue to the killer, had told Deke she knew who he was, and he had said only, "The hell you do." He hadn't shared her excitement. He had seemed taut and unbelieving. He had refused to get rid of that queer couple of his, behaving almost as though he weren't a free agent.

The phone rang and she went into the living room to answer it. Charlie Hammond sounded anxious.

"You all right, Kay?"

"Of course I'm all right. How's your invalid?"

"Two of them now," he said in a tone of resignation. ". . . No, they aren't too uncomfortable. We've got them in isolation up on the third floor, and from the noise they make, they're tearing the place apart. Ran down a nurse at last, a Mrs. Prescott."

"God help you," Kay said feelingly.

"Look, Kay, Sylvia's biting her nails to the quick about you."

"She probably is if she takes anything the Prescott woman says seriously."

"Well, she didn't say much, actually, only stressed your — nervous condition."

"I'm fine," Kay assured him, "and Deke Ransom is on call. His boxer would raise the dead if anyone tried to bother me. There's nothing to worry about."

"The thing is," Charlie said soberly, "the troopers have been up here, asking questions about the accident, about you, about this man you — about Billings. I said we'd never heard of him, that you must have met him after we went abroad. We told them you were absolutely reliable. All that."

"In my right mind," Kay said evenly.

"Well — I wish you were here."

"Thanks, Charlie. Thank Sylvia for me. I'm all right. Honestly I am. If I need anything, I'll sing out."

"If you're sure," Charlie capitulated reluctantly. "But just remember, if anyone tries to give you a hard time, don't wait until you see the whites of his eyes. Shoot first."

She was laughing as she put down the telephone. Sun poured through the windows. Outside Worth was raking leaves. No one could hurt her now. Max came out to slide under the wheel of the Pontiac. For a long time Kay stood at the window, staring at the studio. Deke was working at his easel. Now and then she could see him at the window.

At length she went upstairs to get a notebook and pencil from her handbag, took them out, and found the cuff link she had picked up in Ernest's apartment. She turned it over and over and then laid it gently in her jewel box.

All afternoon she worked steadily, going from room to room, making notes of repairs, redecoration, refurnishing, compiling a list of items to be stored, a larger list of things to donate to the local rummage sale. There would be a still longer list when she ransacked the storeroom. Most of the stuff, of course, was worn-out trash that Paul Forbes could not bear to relinquish, but some of it might be valuable.

Even when darkness fell and she had turned on the lights she was not nervous. She looked in the kitchen and discovered that Mrs. Brundle had prepared a stew that needed only to be heated. There was a salad in the refrigerator, dinner rolls, and fresh gingerbread with whipped cream.

While Kay got out food and turned on the gas under the stew, she wished that she had remembered to buy some liquor in the village. Uncle Paul had given up cocktails several years earlier as an unnecessary indulgence.

When the knock came at the front door, her heart jumped. She put her hand on the chain and hesitated. "Who is it?"

"Mr. Ransom's compliments and he hoped you'd enjoy these with your dinner."

She opened the door for Max, who was carrying a pitcher of martinis and a small carafe of red wine. He nodded in response to her thanks, his eyes searching the lighted hall behind her.

With a chilled martini glass in her hand she went to the telephone. Deke answered at once.

"How nice of you!"

"Did I guess right? There's still a lot I have to learn about your tastes. All serene over there?"

"Of course," she assured him. "Everything is fine."

And everything was all right while she drank two martinis, while she ate the meal Mrs. Brundle had prepared, sipping excellent claret, while she settled in the living room with *The Rector of Justin* and switched on the radio to WQXR.

After a while she was conscious of a vague sort of malaise. She couldn't keep her mind on the book, she didn't know what music she was hearing. All her attention was focused on the dark windows though she would not let herself look toward them. This was ridiculous. No one was watching her. She was imagining things. She was deliberately frightening herself. All she needed was strength of character to shake off her fears. All she needed.

She turned a page, then another, without knowing what she read. She was not listening to the music though she was dimly aware now that her favorite Mozart violin sonata was being played. She was listening for — why, she was listening for Deacon. But Deacon was silent, which meant there was no prowler. No one could get past Deacon. But someone had searched the house. Mrs. Brundle, who was not imaginative, had been sure of that. After so many years she knew the position of every piece of furniture, every book on the shelves. Someone had been there.

It was no use. All right, she told herself angrily, so you're a coward. Face it. She got up to draw the curtains, to shut out the night and whatever loitered in the dark.

She checked the locks, front door, back door, windows, and went upstairs. She'd read in bed for a while. There were lights in the studio but no sign of Deke, no sign of anyone.

For half an hour she determinedly kept her mind on the book and then she gave up, put it down, and began to think about the missing lodger. If she were right, he must be somewhere near at hand, waiting for an opportunity to retrieve the canvas carry-alls.

Willis, or whatever his name was, had had to run for it. And he couldn't run fast with those two cumbersome, heavy bags. She wondered why he had not returned to Mrs. Brundle's house after disposing of them but, of course, he had not known how badly hurt Kay was, how much she would be likely to remember, how soon the hunt would be on.

A sound somewhere made her jump. She tried to relax systematically, arms, legs, jaw. I'm going to sleep, she repeated over and over like an incantation. There was a creak and she lifted her head, listening. Old houses always creak, she told herself. There's nothing wrong. No one could get in, not possibly. You can't afford to panic. If you do anything peculiar, anything like that hysterical outburst you made going down the hill with Mrs. Brundle, they'll have a right to send you to Fenwick. You've got to control yourself.

The band had begun to tighten around her head. The pain struck savagely. Perhaps there was something wrong with her.

An endless half hour passed while Kay lay rigid, wondering if she were going mad with the pain. The clock in the hall began to chime, striking midnight. She gave up then in defeat. For over two weeks she had refused to take the painkiller Dr. Grantling had prescribed for her. She had left the bottle on a kitchen shelf so that, even if she should be unbearably tempted, she would hesitate to go downstairs for it. Now she had come to the limit of her endurance. She switched on the light, pulled on the robe at the foot of the bed, felt for slippers with her bare feet so she would not have to bend over. Walking as

155

softly as possible so as not to jar her head, she went into the hall, groped for the light switch, and started down the stairs. Then, without warning, she was pitching forward on her face. She flung out her hands to break her fall.

She was chilled. That was her first thought. She reached for her blanket, realized in confusion that she was lying head downward. She opened her eyes, dizziness made her swirl through darkness. Next time she opened them she saw that she was lying on the stairs. She tried to move, putting her weight on her hands, and cried out. Her left wrist seemed to be broken.

Later she never knew how long she had lain there. It was the cold more than the pain that eventually forced her to make the effort. It seemed to take hours. She finally accomplished it by letting herself slide, head downward, to the bottom of the staircase. Then, clinging to the banister, she got to her knees, finally to her feet. She hung there until her head cleared. With her right hand against the wall to steady her, switching on lights as she went, she got to the telephone. She set it on the table and dialed and then picked it up awkwardly with her right hand.

Deke answered on the third ring.

"Can you come over?"

"I'm on my way."

Again she repeated her slow progress to the door, fumbled with the bolt and chain and key. There was a tap and a reassuring voice.

"Kay, it's Deke."

She opened the door then. Deke, in dressing gown and coat over his pajamas, looked at her and then said, "Oh, my God!" He picked her up in his arms and put her on the couch. Then, as someone knocked at the door, he said reassuringly, "That will be Max. I left a message for him."

The latter was fully dressed. "Wilma says there is trouble over here. What happened?"

"I don't know yet. I just got here myself. But Miss Forbes has been hurt." He sent Max for warm water and a washcloth and bathed her face and head gently.

"I fell down the stairs," Kay said dully. "I guess I blacked out. I suppose now they'll send me to Fenwick."

"They won't send you anywhere." Deke's hand tightened on her wrist and she moaned. He examined it as gently as he could. "Not broken, I'm pretty sure, but it is probably sprained. We'll have Dr. Grantling look you over."

"I can strap it to relieve the pain," Max said quickly. For a moment he held Deke's eyes in an unspoken message. "I have a kit. Back in a moment."

"What happened?" Deke asked at last. "What made you go downstairs?"

She explained about the racking headache she had been afraid to avow, about the painkiller she had left in the kitchen so it wouldn't be of easy access.

His hands moved along her body, her legs, prodding carefully so as not to hurt her.

"There doesn't seem to be anything broken, but just the same I'll get the doctor up here, no matter what —" He broke off as Max returned. The houseman worked quickly and efficiently, strapping her wrist.

"There," he said at last, "that ought to do the trick, at least for the time being. How did it happen, Miss Forbes?"

She half expected Deke to call him to order but, except for a tightening of the lips, he made no protest.

"She thinks she blacked out on the stairs and fell." The two men exchanged glances and Max went out.

"I'm sorry to be such a nuisance," Kay said.

Deke knelt beside her, one hand touching her cheek lightly. "There are compensations."

From the hallway Max called sharply, "Ransom! Come here."

Deke went out. Kay heard them on the stairs, heard Max say, excitement in his voice, "Take a look at this, will you?"

"I'll be damned!"

"See how it worked? The elastic was stretched across the step, just tacked here against the wall, then when she tripped over it, it rolled up on this side under the banister. Unless someone were looking for it, it wouldn't be visible on this dark staircase."

"But how in hell was it done? How did anyone

get into this place? How did he get past Deacon?"

"I'll take a look around."

"Damn it, you've had your way long enough. She's live bait! I'm going to call the troopers and report this."

Max's voice was a murmur but something of his insistence came through. Deke was protesting, his voice almost inaudible. When he came back into the room, he had a curiously defeated expression. It must be true, then, that Max gave the orders. In any case, it was not the troopers Deke telephoned but Dr. Grantling.

No, he said in answer to the doctor's questions, nothing broken so far as he could tell. Probably she had sprained a wrist but it had been strapped. There were some scratches and some shock, of course.

At the end of what seemed to be a mutually unsatisfactory and irritating conversation, Deke hung up.

"He'll see you in the morning. He has to pay a call at the Hammond house, anyhow."

Seeing his grim expression, Kay asked, "Did he say I'm not competent to be alone?"

Deke evaded a direct answer. "You won't be alone. Max and I will take turns guarding you."

She tried to sit up. "No, that's absurd. I won't have it!" Seeing his stubborn expression, she added quickly, "The whole village would know within twenty-four hours that my tenant was spending the night in the wrong house."

"Oh." He was taken aback. "Okay, we'll keep

you respectable but safe, too."

Again he telephoned. The phone rang for some time.

"Wilma? Miss Forbes had an accident this evening. Will you spend the night over here with her?"

He hung up, scowling, and then smiled at her. "Now I'll take you up to bed. Wilma will be here. Nothing can happen to you." He picked her up, negotiated the narrow staircase cautiously, and set her down on her bed. He leaned forward as though to kiss her and then straightened up with a laugh. "Better not. The patient must be kept quiet. Now where's that painkiller?"

There were voices downstairs, Deke's and Max's and Wilma's. Deke and Wilma came up together. The latter had dressed hastily in slacks and a sweater. Her eyes seemed enormous and blind again. Dope of some kind, Kay thought with a feeling of uneasiness. She swallowed the pills Deke handed her, drank the water.

"There's a bed made up in the room across the hall," Kay said. "This is very kind of you."

Wilma did not look kind. She simply shrugged and said as she left the room, "I'll keep both doors open."

You wouldn't hear the last trump, Kay thought, but she made no comment.

CHAPTER 12

Kay raised heavy lids, looked at the bedside clock. Half-past eight. She'd have to get up to admit Mrs. Brundle. Her eyes fell on her strapped wrist and memories of the night came flooding back. Someone had set a trap for her on the stairs, a trap meant to leave no trace, or perhaps to be removed before anyone checked. There was to be an accident for which Kay herself was responsible, one that would either kill her or force Dr. Grantling to put her in Fenwick.

Ernest's killer was near at hand, able to enter a locked and bolted house as he pleased, and in spite of Deacon. Last night Deacon had not made a sound.

No one gets past Deacon, Deke had said. Oh, yeah? It was after Deke's arrival at the studio that the house had been searched. When she had asked awkward questions, he had distracted her attention by making love to her. Well, he'd been successful at that, she thought savagely. Always wrong about people, Charlie Hammond had said. Always wrong.

And Deke took orders from his houseman. He refused to get rid of him, to get rid of Wilma who might be, possibly was, a dope addict. Max had — where had Max been last night? He had been fully clothed when he reached the house. Apparently Deke had left a message for him. Had Max been setting the trap on the staircase?

Live bait, Deke had said. Live bait. But he hadn't called the troopers. He'd been ordered not to.

She sat up in bed and was aware of a curious sense of well being for a girl who had so nearly broken her neck the night before. There was no trace of her headache.

"That stuff must really work," Wilma said from the doorway, as though echoing her thoughts. "Not a sound out of you all night."

Kay stretched. "I hope you got some sleep."

"I take sleeping pills," Wilma said bluntly. This morning she looked very young, like a schoolgirl except for her expression. There was no hope in her face, no expectation.

"Aren't you afraid of them?"

"It's that or go crazy. They help you forget for a time."

Kay smiled. "You're too young to have much to forget."

"I guess it depends on the kind of person you are. Some people just don't give a damn. People like you. Off with the old, on with the new."

Seeing the bitter unhappiness in the girl's face, Kay made no retort. She reached for her robe and slid her legs out of bed, saw the bruises on one knee, the skinned gash on the shinbone. It had bled a lot.

Wilma saw it, too. "Marked you up a bit,

didn't it?" She did not seem to be displeased. "I'll bring you some coffee before I go. How do you like it?"

"Black, please. There's some instant, I use it mornings as a rule when I'm alone."

When Wilma had gone, Kay dropped robe and nightgown and examined herself in the full-length mirror. There was a skinned patch on her left cheekbone, a big purple bruise on her left hip, her left leg bruised and skinned, her left wrist stiff and the fingers swollen. This was the third attempt.

She took a sponge bath and dressed awkwardly. She was brushing her hair when Wilma came in with a cup of coffee.

She set it on the dressing table. "Instant, as you said. Mrs. Brundle can make you some real coffee when she gets your breakfast. I'm no cook."

And if you're not a cook, Kay wondered when the sullen girl had taken an abrupt departure, just what are you doing here? All she was sure of was that Deke had lied to her.

Absently she stirred the coffee to dissolve it. There was a gritty sound. She stirred again, raised the spoon, letting the coffee drip off, saw the glitter. Then she ran her finger over the coffee spoon, felt the tiny pricks. Ground glass.

When she could steady herself, she put the cup carefully on the floor of her closet, locked the door and pocketed the key. Wilma. It was Wilma who had put ground glass in the coffee. A fourth attempt to kill her. But why? Why? The money, of course.

There was only one thing she was sure of. The money wasn't hidden in the house. She had searched every inch of it. And the killer knew as well as she did that it wasn't there.

She walked up and down the room. Dr. Grantling would not believe her. The troopers would not believe her. Deke — but Deke had brought Max and Wilma with him. Deke wouldn't, or couldn't, help.

Her mind went round like an animal in a cage. She could tell the Hammonds, but she would only worry them. They couldn't come to her and she couldn't go to them.

Malcolm Stoddard? He had seen the slash in her fur cape. That, at least, he had believed. He would do something. At least he could return Deke Ransom's check and force him to move out. But what had brought Deke to the studio in the first place? He had learned about it through his brother, at least, that was what he said.

Mrs. Brundle's jeep came in with the usual uproar, and in a few minutes Kay heard her bustling around in the kitchen. She went down the stairs, this time warily, testing every step. There was no trace of the elastic that had been stretched across a step. Max or Deke must have removed it.

If this goes on, she thought, I'll be afraid of everything.

Mrs. Brundle looked at her, saw the mark on

her cheek, the strapped wrist. "Looks like you had a fall."

Remembering Nelly, Kay said, "I tripped on the stairs."

"Who strapped your wrist?"

"Mr. Ransom's houseman."

"You sure got acquainted right away, didn't you? Nelly was saying just last night it was nice for you having an important man, and unmarried too, right next door. Mr. Weeks — you know him, owns our daily paper — was saying on the telephone that public relations men try to get Mr. Ransom to do stories about their clients, but he's mighty independent. He does what he likes and only what interests him. Nice-looking man, I thought."

After a pause she suggested, "I guess you had one of those dizzy spells." When Kay made no answer, Mrs. Brundle examined her shrewdly. "You're walking kind of stiff."

"I skinned my knee and bruised my hip."

"You ought to be more careful. You could hurt yourself real bad that way."

Kay began to laugh and then found it difficult to stop.

"You sit down here. Coffee's ready and you'll have breakfast in a couple of minutes." As the housekeeper set the coffee before Kay, she asked casually, "Have you seen Dr. Grantling recently?"

"He's supposed to come around this morning."

"That's good. Maybe he could give you some of them tranquilizers to quiet you down. You're just about hysterical. What's wrong with that coffee? It's the same as I always make it. The way you keep filling the spoon and letting the coffee dribble back into the cup. I declare there are times when you act downright queer, Kay."

"Suppose," Kay said, goaded beyond endurance, "you confine yourself to your housework, Mrs. Brundle. If you can't do that, I'm afraid you'll have to look for another job."

There was a dead silence in the kitchen. At last Mrs. Brundle, sounding bewildered, said, "I've known you since you was a little girl, Kay, and you've never spoke to me like that. All I want is what's best for you. But if you think," her voice — quivered with indignation, "I've stepped out of my place —"

"Sorry." Kay abandoned the unequal struggle.

"That's all right," Mrs. Brundle forgave her handsomely. "You're only unreasonable because of that poor head of yours. You've always been nice to me. Nice-spoken. Only just lately you've got more like your uncle. Sharp-like. But then you do something real nice like giving my lodger a job. He was mighty pleased. Maybe he'll get a little color and have more stamina now. Nelly was saying just last night —"

Kay pushed back her chair. "I won't be long. Keep my breakfast hot for me, will you?"

She put on a coat and started across the lawn. Max was lifting a piece of glass off the ground.

He set it down when he saw her, looked her over quickly.

"I hope you feel all right this morning."

"A little stiff but that's the extent of the damage. Thank you for strapping my wrist." As he nodded without comment, she asked, "What on earth are you doing to my basement window?"

"That," Max told her, "is where your intruder got in last night. Smashed the window, got into the basement, came up the cellar stairs."

"But the door to the kitchen from the cellar is kept bolted."

"It wasn't when I looked at it last night, Miss Forbes."

Standing facing him, her hands thrust into her coat pockets, Kay said, "It's odd, isn't it that anyone could get past Deacon. He never made a sound."

"He'll never make another sound," Max said roughly. "He was poisoned last night."

"Oh, no!" Kay cried in protest.

"I'm going to bury him as soon as I put in this new pane of glass for you. All I hope is that I can finish the job before Wilma finds the poor beast. That will just about provide the finishing touch."

"Wilma?"

"Deacon was her dog."

"But she wouldn't kill her own dog!" Kay exclaimed.

Max stared at her. "How did you come to think

of a thing like that?"

"Then there must be two of you in it."

Max took a step toward her. "What is that supposed to mean?"

Kay stood her ground. "Someone tried to kill me."

"That," he said patiently, as though addressing an extraordinarily dull child, "is why I am replacing the windowpane."

"I don't mean that trap on the stairs last night. This morning Wilma brought me a cup of coffee. There was ground glass in it."

Max stood stock-still, his expression changing ludicrously.

"I've locked it up where no one can get it," Kay said clearly. "It's evidence."

"Yes," he said, "yes, of course. But Wilma — hell, I suppose it's possible, what with one thing and another."

"What's wrong with Wilma?"

"Oh, it's on account of Ransom, of course. You and Ransom." Max spoke almost absently, as though he were thinking of something else. "But one thing is impossible. Wilma wouldn't have killed Deacon."

"If you ask me, she's half nuts."

"But people say that about you too, Miss Forbes," Max said pleasantly. "Just look at this thing reasonably. If Wilma wanted to break into this house, she wouldn't have needed to kill Deacon."

"Maybe she thought I'd figure it that way

myself, or if I was too stupid to do so, you could point it out to me."

Max grinned. "I'm not all that Machiavellian." He sobered. "I'll tell Ransom about the coffee as soon as he wakes up. He was on guard duty outside your house all night. I'll take over to-night."

"That won't be necessary. I am sorry that I must ask Mr. Ransom to give up his lease on the studio at once. I'll return his check."

For once Max was frankly dismayed. He stared at her in open consternation. "Miss Forbes, please wait until you have talked to Ransom. I can't tell you how important it is."

"Of course, Four hundred thousand dollars."

"All I ask is that you talk to him first. Maybe he can persuade you where I can't."

"He's a good persuader," Kay said dryly.

"Kay," Mrs. Brundle called. "Telephone."

It was Sylvia Hammond. "Darling, what goes on over there? Dr. Grantling just came to see our invalids — all three of them now — and said he'd stop at your house in half an hour. He told us you'd had an accident and that Mr. Ransom had called him."

"I fell down the stairs," Kay said. "Just a few bruises. No damage done."

"But Mr. Ransom said —"

"It's all right, really it is, Sylvia. And tell Dr. Grantling I won't need him." Kay switched quickly to the chickenpox invasion.

"Isn't it just like Charlie?" Sylvia wailed. "He

hadn't seen any of this miserable tribe in years and barely knew them anyhow, and doesn't even like them, for heaven's sake! But the mother wrote a touching letter about the children being in poor health and having no money. So what does my crazy husband do but suggest we trot home and harbor them until they are well."

"And what," Kay laughed, "does crazy Sylvia do but agree."

"Well, you know the line, 'Thy people shall be my people,' no matter what the trials and tribulations. This bitter cup I'll drain to the last drop."

"You're the happiest pair in the world, so don't give me that."

"I know. I still pinch myself to see if it's real. If you could only find someone just like Charlie —"

"Is there anyone like him?"

"Oh, a reasonable facsimile. You're sure you are all right, Kay? I'm glad Deke Ransom is so near. Of all the fascinating —"

There was a confused jumble of voices and then Charlie said, "You'd better marry this guy Ransom, Kay, and take him out of circulation before he breaks up my home."

Kay laughed. "Any time that happens!"

The corn muffins were piping hot and this time Kay drank the coffee without inspecting it. She had just finished breakfast when Dr. Grantling arrived.

"Oh, I'm sorry, Doctor. I told Mrs. Hammond that you needn't call."

"She must have forgotten to tell me." The doctor was bland. "But now I'm here I might as well have a look at you."

He examined the sprained wrist, flexed the fingers of the swollen hand, restrapped it, dug in his bag for a sling.

"You'll be more comfortable wearing this. Whoever strapped it knew his job." He prodded the deep bruise on her hip. "Lucky you didn't smash that. Dizzy spell? Did you black out?"

"I — there was a hole in the stair carpet and I caught my heel on it."

"You'll have to do better than that, Miss Forbes. I've been up and down those stairs twenty times at least and I looked for things like that because your uncle had to use the stairs."

Kay made no comment.

"Lucky that Mr. Ransom was on the spot."

"I called him."

He nodded, sat back looking at her. "I had a long talk with Mr. Stoddard. He and I disagree about — certain measures."

"Like Fenwick?"

"Like Fenwick," he agreed. "I still think you'd be better off if you had a month up there."

"Last time you mentioned a week."

Dr. Grantling ignored her comment. "It's a pleasant place. The food is gourmet all the way, as they say in the commercials. The grounds are attractive."

"There is nothing wrong with my mind."

"Then something else is damned wrong," the doctor said bluntly.

"Leave it to Mr. Stoddard. I promised him that I wouldn't fight if he decided I should be in Fenwick."

"Stoddard's judgment might not be quite detached."

"Why on earth not?"

Somewhat to her surprise, Dr. Grantling was embarrassed. "Well, you're a very attractive young woman and you have an extremely persuasive way with you. Make it hard for a man to say no."

Kay chuckled. "If you think for a moment that Mr. Stoddard is attracted to me! Why, he must be sixty. He was my father's friend. Besides, he's married."

"I'm fifty-five. I'm married. I also have four children. But I am highly conscious of the fact that you are the most alluring female I've ever seen. Now if you want to report me for unprofessional conduct —"

Kay leaned back in her chair and laughed. "You know, Doctor, I suspect you of being highly professional. The modern method of cheering up the patient, building up her morale."

His eyes twinkled as he picked up his bag. "I won't be back unless you send for me. You'll be stiff for a few days and you'll notice that bruised hip more tomorrow than you do today. In fact, you'll discover a lot of muscles you never knew you had, and they'll all be sore. But," he grinned at her, "I think you'll live."

"I hope so," Kay said fervently.

CHAPTER 13

"I was thinking, Kay," Mrs. Brundle hovered in the doorway, ready to leave, "if you want to invite your tenant to supper some night I could fix something real nice for you. Give him an idea of my cooking. There's a casserole in the icebox for you. Just heat it up."

"Mr. Ransom won't be staying long enough for that."

"Nelly said he'd be here at least three months."

"How does Nelly know?"

"Well, you know how these party lines are. She heard Mrs. Weeks talking to someone, Nelly couldn't catch the voice, saying her husband had interviewed him for next week's paper. He didn't drop a word about going. Said he was going to paint."

When Kay made no comment, the housekeeper flounced indignantly out and a moment later the jeep started with its customary explosions.

Worth did not appear until nearly midafternoon. He trundled out the heavy gasoline lawn mower and started on the high grass. Pushing it seemed to take all his strength, and Kay was half inclined to tell him to stop. However, he had been eager to have both the job and the money, and probably to escape from Nelly's tender ministrations as well. They, Kay admitted, would be enough to smother any man. The motor stopped and Kay went to the window. Worth was looking across the lawn toward the studio. It was a moment before she saw what had attracted his attention. Max, a spade over his shoulder, was walking toward the studio. Behind him Wilma stumbled, sobbing aloud like a child.

A few minutes later Max came out to get into the Pontiac. Kay slipped on her coat and walked swiftly toward the studio before her courage failed her. As she passed the big studio window she saw Deke holding Wilma in his arms, looking down at her with an expression of compassionate tenderness.

Because of you and Ransom, of course, Max had said. Kay was about to turn back when Deke looked up, saw her, released Wilma, speaking to her quietly. The girl ran out of the room and Deke opened the door before Kay could escape.

"Come in, Kay."

She hesitated and then went into the studio. The unfinished sketch of her head still stood on the easel, but no more work had been done on it.

He looked at the sling. "How are you feeling?"

"A little stiff but otherwise all right."

"Sit down, won't you. Don't just hover there." Laughter edged his voice.

Kay sat down and accepted the cigarette he offered her. When the silence seemed about to last forever, she said, "Max tells me you were on guard all night. That was very kind of you, but it wasn't in the bond, you know."

"Locking the stable! You heard what happened to Deacon?"

"Max told me. What a filthy thing to do!"

"A particularly filthy thing. Wilma's all broken up about it."

"So I — noticed."

He smiled at her. "So you did." The smile faded. "Look here, Kay, Max thinks you have some idea that Wilma put ground glass in your coffee this morning."

"More of my wild imagination, perhaps. But I have the coffee cup under lock and key."

"Are you sure about the ground glass?"

"Positive."

"You didn't drink any of it?" He was alarmed.

She shook her head. "I noticed that something was wrong so I didn't touch it."

"What do you intend to do with it?"

"Turn it over to Mr. Stoddard." There was a deliberate challenge in her voice.

"That's a good idea. What did you do with the jar of instant coffee?"

"Why, I suppose it's still in the kitchen. You don't think I intend to use it again!"

"No, but you ought to lock that up, too. And do be careful about handling it. Not that there's much chance of finding any fingerprints."

"But it was Wilma." She was bewildered. "Even Max thinks so."

He shook his head. "No," he said definitely, "it wasn't Wilma. You can get that idea out of your head."

"Who then?" she insisted. "Why did it happen? That trap on the stairs last night, the coffee this morning. Why?"

"There are four hundred thousand dollars at stake," he reminded her, "and you have broadcast far and wide that you could identify the murderer. Those are two pretty sound reasons. What interests me is using the instant coffee. Do you drink it often?"

"Mornings, as a rule, when I'm in a hurry."

"Mrs. Brundle doesn't make it for you?"

She shook her head.

"Who would know about your habits?"

"Anyone who knows me, I suppose. You mention trivial things like that. But what difference —" she began impatiently.

"The process of elimination. But after this we'll see that nothing happens to you."

Kay pressed out the cigarette, taking her time. She looked up to meet his eyes steadily. "Sorry, I am writing Mr. Stoddard today — I'd have called if it weren't for the party line — to instruct him to return your check and ask you to leave here at once. I hope, knowing my wishes, you won't wait for that. I'd like you to go immediately. Today, if possible."

She could read nothing in his face. There had been only an involuntary stiffening of his body.

"I can't go, Kay."

"Why not? I don't want you here."

"I understand that."

"Then —"

"You wouldn't like the truth if I told you. And right now I can't tell you. Max —"

"Who is Max? He's no houseman. He's never in his life been in a subordinate position. He doesn't even know how to act the part."

"Max is the man who gives the orders."

"And Wilma?" When he did not answer, she went on, "I assumed at first your couple would be man and wife. But she's not a cook, she said so herself, and I don't think she is Max's wife."

"No, she —" He broke off. "Look here, Kay, there's so much at stake and so little I can tell you. All I can promise is that you will be protected. If you could just trust me." He came to cup her chin in his hand and tilt back her head. "Is that too difficult?"

"I can tell you one thing, Deke, if it's the money you are looking for, you won't find it in the house. I've searched every inch of the place from the cellar to the attic."

He released her abruptly. When he spoke again, his voice was impersonal. "Then let's look at the matter logically. We assume the thief came back here with those carry-alls after staging the accident at the ravine and disposing of the body of the man he had killed."

"There's no place else he could have gone in the time."

He nodded. "That's the way we figured it. The

money isn't in the house. As the ground was covered with snow, it couldn't be buried outside. So that leaves the studio." He reached for her sound hand, drew her to her feet. "Let's go look for it. I've had a lot of varied experiences in my time, but I've never gone looking for buried treasure."

Again she searched his face, but there was nothing to read. Big as the studio was, the room provided no place for concealment except under the couch. Kay, wincing as she knelt to peer under it because of her skinned knees, had the impression that, behind his sober face, Deke was laughing at her.

One of the two bedrooms upstairs was being used, to judge by the clothing, by Deke. He waited impassively while she searched it, opening bureau drawers for her and taking out suitcases. When he had tapped on the door of the other bedroom, there was a muffled sound and he opened it. Wilma was lying across the bed, sobbing.

"What do you want?" she asked without looking up.

"Just searching for buried treasure," he said dryly, and Kay's face burned. None the less she followed him into the room, looked in the small closet and under the bed. Wilma did not move until the door had closed behind them.

Max, Kay realized, must be sleeping on the couch in the big studio. The bathroom required only a minute. The kitchen, because of its cupboards, took longer. There was no basement. Nothing remained except the storeroom.

"I forgot the key," she said; "I'll go back."

Deke turned the knob and the door opened. He stood back for her to go in. Peering into the dark room, she hesitated. "There's a drop light in the center. I — there are rats."

He moved away and in a moment an unshaded drop light came on. Kay, who had started to go in, drew back her foot hastily. She had brushed against a trap holding a dead rat.

"Okay, stay where you are," Deke said. "I'll get rid of the body before you go in."

She averted her eyes as he went past her with the trap and its dangling victim. She heard the door of the incinerator open and close and after a few minutes he returned, the trap reset and baited.

"All right, nothing to frighten you now. They're cowardly creatures unless they are cornered. If there are any more around, they'll be as anxious to avoid you as you are to avoid them." When she did not enter the storeroom, he turned, holding out his hand. "Come on, Kay, it's all right now."

"There's not much point in looking any farther, is there?"

"What do you mean?"

"I mean you've been in here before. That unlocked door, the rat trap —"

"Max wanted to get rid of the rats and I needed extra space to store my canvases. Remember?"

"I remember." She came into the room slowly, looking from the canvases stacked against the wall to the clutter of furniture, discarded bedsteads, chairs with broken springs, lamps, boxes labeled. "Grandfather's letters written during the Civil War," "Jennie's wedding dress," "Pictures taken during Ralph's grand tour," "Walter's stamp collection," "Canceled checks — 1922–1944."

The canvas carry-alls were under two faded Persian rugs in which moths and rodents had left their traces. Deke dragged the bags out, one at a time. There was a queer look on his face.

"I never thought we'd find them. Well, thank God for that much! What do you want done with them, Kay?"

She started to look at her watch, remembered that she had not been able to put it on because of the strapping. "What time is it?"

"A few minutes after three."

"Too late for the local bank. I don't know what's best to do."

Deke smiled. "It looks as though we'll have to do guard duty on these too, tonight, only I don't particularly like dividing our forces. Apparently there are two choices: you can stay here — you can have my room — or we'll take the bags over to the house. Which would you prefer?"

Kay was looking at the nearest bag. "It's different, not quite the same shape. It was bulging." She leaned over. Before Deke's quick gesture could stop her, she pulled the zipper, lifted out a handful of crumpled newspaper.

A rat slithered along the wall and Kay said dully, "Let's get out of here." She straightened up awkwardly, the arm in the sling made balancing difficult, stumbled against a canvas, which fell with a clatter. She stared in disbelief at the portrait of the young man with the long pointed upper lip. Behind her Deke was terribly intent, close enough to touch.

"That," he said levelly, "is my brother Dan."

Fast as she ran, he caught up with her before she had crossed the studio.

"Wait, Kay, you can't go like that. You've got to listen."

She let him lead her back to the couch without struggling, refused a cigarette. At last she made herself look at him. He seemed terribly tired.

"Are you all in it together?" she asked. Something in his expression reproached her. "But what can I think? What am I to believe?"

"Do you believe I tried to kill you; that I would ever, under any circumstances, have been a party to hurting you?" When she made no reply, he said, "Do you, Kay?"

"Deke, I —"

He took her in his arms, rocking her gently. "All right, dear. It's been a nightmare for you too, I realize that." He raised her head at last, kissed her gently, released her.

"For me too? Oh, you mean your brother." Belated understanding flooded her. "That's why you came here. To find him. To — stop him."

But there could be only one end for Dan Ransom. He had killed Ernest and Uncle Paul. He had tried four times to kill her. There was nothing she could say to comfort Deke and, at the moment, that seemed to be the most pressing need. She put up her good hand to touch his cheek, to smooth the deep lines in his forehead. "But, darling, if he has already taken the money, he won't be back." When he made no comment, she demanded, "Would he?"

"You've forgotten," he said heavily, "that you can identify the murderer. So, if you are to be safe, he has to be found."

A car door slammed and he got up. "That's Max."

"Deke, is Max — that is, does he know Dan? Is he working with him?"

"In a way."

"And they've just been using you, or were you trying to find your brother, to protect him?"

The door opened and Max came in, looked from Kay to Deke, and shook his head. "No luck."

Deke walked across to the house with Kay. She paused to speak to Worth, who was trudging across the lawn behind the heavy mower. "Better knock off for the day. Don't do too much until you're more accustomed to it."

"Thanks, I believe I will." He mopped his bald head. "It's a long time since I've had such a workout."

Deke insisted on examining every room for booby traps. She had never suspected that a house with which she was so familiar could offer so many pitfalls. He checked the lamps and the wall plugs, investigated the gas fireplace in the unused living room, went over the staircase with a flashlight.

"What happened to the elastic band that tripped me last night?"

"Max took it. He also replaced the basement windowpane and put a chain on the door that leads from the kitchen to the basement. Nobody will get in that way again."

In the kitchen he took the jar of instant coffee, picking it up with tongs and dropping it into a plastic bag.

"What about dinner?" he demanded.

She opened the refrigerator. "Mrs. Brundle made me a casserole."

"Don't eat it. Have you any eggs? Stick to those for tonight. I'll send over a cocktail and I'll show up about nine."

"Why?"

"I'm going to spend the night in your living room, and if that starts the gossips talking, let them talk. I'll promise to make an honest woman of you."

"But, Deke —"

He kissed her lightly and went back to the studio. Kay watched him until he was out of sight. He had walked, she thought, as though he were very tired.

Only when she was alone did some kind of sanity return. When she was with Deke she didn't seem able to think straight, which was humiliating. Now she remembered what she had learned. The murderer was Deke's brother. Max was his partner and he had been using Deke as a cover, employing what pressures she could not guess. The money was gone. Had it been taken by Max or by Deke's brother Dan?

While she boiled eggs, she remembered Wilma in Deke's arms. That night she poured out her cocktail untasted.

CHAPTER 14

"The Marines to the rescue," Deke said when Kay opened the door for him. When he had surveyed her carefully, he shook his head. "Every time I leave you, all your distrust comes surging back. What am I to do about you, Kay?" As she made a quick gesture, he dropped the arm he had put around her. "As bad as that? How am I going to teach you not to be afraid, my darling?"

When she failed to answer, he said, "Why don't you go up to bed? You had a bad time last night. And don't worry. No one will get past me."

"That," she reminded him, "is what you said about Deacon."

His face hardened. "Poor little devil. And poor Wilma. She was still crying when I sent her up to bed."

"And doped to the hilt," Kay remarked coldly.

"That won't become a habit. Just a kind of cushion until she gets over the worst of it. After all, they were married only five months ago." As Kay gave a startled exclamation, he said, "Yes, she is Dan's wife. We didn't want her to come here, but she got in such a frenzy that it seemed easier at the time. Now I don't know. If I could have guessed about Deacon — that's my name, by the way, but it sounds a shade pontifical so I've been Deke since I was a kid. Dan gave the boxer to Wilma when they were married."

"It's because of you and Ransom, of course," Max had said. Oh, God, Kay thought in despair, if I only knew what to believe!

As though reading her thoughts, Deke said, "You are wrong about Wilma, you know. She's just a kid, heartbroken and lost. She would never have pulled that stunt with the coffee, Kay. She's incapable of it."

"She doesn't like me," Kay said flatly.

"She's resentful. I don't quite know how to put this."

"It isn't necessary."

"Yes, I think it is. You've got some odd notions, as I've been learning lately. The thing with Wilma is that she is perfectly aware of what is happening between us, and don't ask me what that is. And because she feels right now that her own life is finished, she can't forgive us for starting to rebuild a life together. That's what we are doing, isn't it?"

"Is it?" Kay asked.

"Go get some rest," he advised her. "Max is watching in the studio. He's armed too."

"Too!"

Deke looked chagrined. "I hadn't meant to tell you. I thought it would make you nervous." Rather sheepishly he removed an automatic from his pocket.

"A gun," Kay said slowly, "against your own

brother? You're expecting him to come back tonight, aren't you?"

Deke stood staring out of the window into the darkness. At length he said, "Dan won't come here. I know where he is. Not far away, as a matter of fact. He is buried in your family plot."

A moment passed before his meaning registered. "You're out of your mind! That's Ernest. There couldn't conceivably have been a mistake. Mrs. Brundle identified him."

"How could she?" Deke asked quietly. "By the time the fire had burned out there was — so little." After a pause he went on, his voice impersonal again. "Of course, there were things — his teeth, probably other evidence — but at that time no one thought of an exchange. The accident had seemed to be quite straightforward."

Kay sat down, dazed. "Are you trying to tell me that Ernest is a thief? That he is a murderer? Ernest? But why, Deke. Why?"

"Four hundred thousand dollars," he reminded her.

"Ernest! But he never even knew about the money until just before we left the house. No one knew except for Uncle Paul."

"And Dan. What had you intended to do with it?"

"Put it in a bank at the first possible moment."

"Did Billings agree with that?"

Kay started to speak. "He — I'm so bewildered — so — but why did he have to kill?"

"Dan was a Treasury agent. So is Max, of

course. And, by the way, Max found your money and it is safe in the local bank vault. He has a receipt for you, but he didn't want to tell you." He pulled it out of his billfold, handed it to her. "You're a very indiscreet person, you know." He gave her a detached, affectionate smile. "He thought if you knew the situation you would betray your knowledge in one of your trusting moments. We haven't, as you have probably noticed, seen eye to eye on this thing. I wanted you to get out of here. Max wanted you to stay."

"Live bait!"

"I know," he admitted. "I don't like it any better than you do, but I've been more or less helpless. Max needed me as cover and I was glad enough to play along on Dan's account, but Max hasn't given me much of a free hand."

Kay shook her head as though trying to clear it. "I can't understand anything. Do you mean it was all planned?"

"No, I think it was spur of the minute. This fellow Billings walked into a fantastic setup, four hundred thousand dollars in currency that you intended to put in the bank, declare to the government, take out of circulation. I suppose the temptation was more than he could withstand."

He added, watching her carefully, trying to be scrupulously fair, "I'd hate to know how many people would have felt an irresistible desire to get their hands on that money. Practically in his pocket and you hell-bent on doing the right

189

thing. It would be a terrific temptation."

The troopers had assumed that Kay had rammed the Cadillac and sent it into the ravine, but they had not blamed her. The road was treacherous and the Ford's brakes had been useless.

"Why were they?" Kay asked. "You asked me that, you remember."

Deke gave her an uneasy look. He shrugged his shoulders. Dan had halted the Cadillac and Billings had had no intention of letting the money get away from him. He had struck Dan down. Because of the poor visibility Kay had not seen which man had been hurt. She had seen what she expected to see. Billings discovered that Paul Forbes was dead and Kay was unconscious. He removed the money, sent the Cadillac into the ravine with Dan in it, and set fire to the car. Then he got the hell out.

Obviously the whole thing was unpremeditated or he would have provided an escape hatch. Instead, he had no place to go but back up the road. The sound of the crash, the sight of the flames had brought an immediate response. He was caught. He had hidden the money in the storeroom of the studio and cleared out until he could get it away in safety and in less conspicuous carriers.

"But if it is Ernest, he's still here, still near at hand. He can get in this house. That booby trap on the stairs, the coffee this morning. Where is he, Deke? Where is he?"

"I wish to God I knew so we could end this nightmare. About all we know — Max and the government boys — is that he either got back into his New York apartment one night or he has a confederate who acted for him, someone who removed his belongings and wiped off his fingerprints. And that, Max tells me, was a highly professional job. It's almost impossible for a person who has lived in a place three months not to leave at least a few fingerprints, however careful a job of cleaning up has been done. You'd be surprised at the number of things you touch in the course of a day, not just the obvious things like light switches and doorknobs, but the wall, furniture, glasses and dishes and kettles and bathroom fixtures."

"Deke, that subway accident, the knife —"

He nodded grimly.

She tried to summon up a picture of Ernest and found it impossible. There were little things, his charm, his confidence, the wide sweeping gestures, the sun-tanned face, the flashing smile, the way he could make her laugh, the crisp dark hair. That was all, really, she had ever known of him. But what she had known she had liked. She came back to that.

"You can't really prove any of this, can you, Deke? That your brother is in Ernest's grave. That Ernest is a thief and a murderer."

"Max thinks we can — with your help."

She was stiff with resistance. "I'm not a bloodhound," she said hotly.

191

"Take it easy, Kay. You aren't going to be dragged screaming into anything. But I should think, for your own peace of mind, you'd like to be sure."

"Well?"

"There's one thing at least we can check out. Dan's identity. Even though the Brundles moved his things, there are bound to be fingerprints. Those would establish his presence there."

Of course, the fact that Dan had never appeared at the Forbes house when Mrs. Brundle was around was evidence of a negative sort that he was her missing lodger, but Max wanted proof that Dan was the man in the grave, and that he had been murdered. The Treasury boys didn't like it, Deke explained, his voice colorless, when one of their men was killed.

"Well?" Kay said again.

"Dan had no motive for killing Billings, Kay. His only objective was to see that Paul Forbes was paying his taxes. But Dan disappeared."

"So," Kay reminded him, "did Ernest."

Deke was making rapid sketches, tearing them out of his notebook.

"He's not far away," he said at last. "That's about all we know."

She drew a long breath. "It's Ernest you are waiting for — with that gun."

"He's a man who came from nowhere, Kay. No army record. No passport. Except for his apartment there's no trace of his existence. No bank account. So obviously there never was a man named Ernest Billings. Do you have a picture of him?"

Kay shook her head. She didn't have a thing except for the cuff link she had found under the edge of the couch in his apartment. When she had explained, she went upstairs to get it from her jewel box.

"It had rolled under the edge of the couch and I found it when I was looking for my lipstick. I think it is something he valued, because he was so late that morning. He said he had been hunting for a lost cuff link."

Deke looked it over and dropped it in an envelope which he sealed.

"Will you help us, Kay?"

"What do you want me to do?"

What he wanted, he said, was to have Kay arrange to clear the Brundle house so that Max could examine Dan's belongings and look for fingerprints. He couldn't do it openly, with Nelly serving as a broadcasting station. If Ernest Billings should be anywhere in reach of a party line, he would hear all about it within a matter of hours and he would disappear.

"Even without trying to retrieve the money?" Kay asked dryly.

"At a risk of spending the rest of his life in prison? I don't see him taking that chance."

"But Ernest likes taking risks," Kay said suddenly. "Challenges. Excitement. He said," she paused for a moment, "he said, when he asked me to marry him, that I was a calculated risk."

He nodded thoughtfully. "Of course. Your judgment of people is terrible," he smiled at her, "but your integrity is rock-bottom." He added, "He must have been very much in love with you to take that risk." When she made no comment, he asked, "How bad is this for you, Kay?"

"I don't know. I can't take it in. I can't readjust my thinking, my picture of Ernest. I can't — oh, I can understand the temptation of the money, perhaps. But not the killing. Lots of people would steal if it were easy, especially when so much money was involved and practically without risk. But to kill your brother, to put the Ford's brakes out of commission — that means, doesn't it, that he never intended me to take that money to New York. He hoped I'd die on the incline. The knife on the subway platform, the booby trap on the stairs, the ground glass — oh, dear God! It's a nightmare."

"That's why we have to get him now, Kay. You won't be safe until we do. It's dangerous to know a murderer."

After a long time she asked, "What do you want me to do, Deke?"

She might, he suggested, take Nelly for a long drive the next afternoon. Worth would be occupied with the gardening.

"I haven't a car," she reminded him.

"You can take the Pontiac."

"No, Deke, I can't drive again. I can't!" She added, "I'd rather die."

"It might come to that." He did not attempt

to persuade her, he simply waited.

At last she said, "I'll call Nelly in the morning."

If he was relieved, he made no sign of it. "Good, that's settled then."

"But what about Mrs. Brundle? She is always in her own house in the afternoons."

"She is going to have an extra job tomorrow, helping Mrs. Weeks prepare for a big tea party."

"How do you know?"

Deke grinned. "I had a talk with Weeks, but not over the telephone. So that clears the decks."

"You felt awfully sure of me," she said resentfully.

He was wise enough to make no comment.

CHAPTER 15

Sometime toward morning Kay fell into an exhausted sleep. Much of the night she had stared into the darkness trying to absorb the fact that Ernest Billings was a thief and a murderer, that he had made four deliberate attempts to kill her. Part of the time she accepted it, part of the time she rejected it.

Ernest, with whom she had shared so much laughter, had tried to drive a knife into her back. No, it was impossible. She was a calculated risk, he had told her. She tossed restlessly. It couldn't be possible. But Deke believed that it was his brother Dan, and not Ernest Billings, who lay in the new grave on the hill. She had not yet gone to the cemetery with its two fresh mounds. It was too far to walk and she hadn't wanted Mrs. Brundle's company when she went there.

Now and then she heard Deke walking quietly through the house. The smell of tobacco drifted up the stairs. Deke was on guard. Or was he? Friend or foe?

But, she remembered, he had given her a receipt for the money, which was now safely in the bank. Somehow, at the time, the fact had hardly registered. And that meant, didn't it, that Deke was all right.

She found herself indulging in an unproductive effort to compare Deke with Ernest, to balance their qualities. It didn't work, of course. What counted was one's personal reaction to people. *Always wrong,* Charlie had said. But if she had been wrong about John, as Charlie believed; if she had been wrong about Ernest, as Deke believed; she could be equally wrong about Deke himself.

Ernest found life exciting, challenging, he felt that he proved something to himself by taking risks, even if they were pointless risks. Deke was involved in mankind. He probed constantly, seeking for — what had he called it? — approximate truth about people. But what, she wondered in despair, did it all add up to? She had accepted John because he needed her. She had been attracted to Ernest because she needed him. But Deke? He was too adult to be satisfied with a relationship that involved either dependency or a power struggle.

Across the lawn, in the darkened studio, Max was alert, waiting for Ernest to come for the money. And upstairs Wilma was waiting for nothing. Nothing any more. Kay understood now the girl's bitter hostility. While her own life seemed to have ended, she saw Kay and Deke absorbed in each other, enraptured by that first moment of the recognition of love.

She hadn't, Kay realized, felt like that about Ernest. She recalled now the odd hesitation she had experienced when he asked her to marry him, an awareness that her future with this man would be an unknown quantity.

Mrs. Brundle's jeep awakened her. She put on a robe and went hastily downstairs to make sure that Deke had left no evidence of his presence there during the night. She shook up a pillow on the couch, emptied an ashtray, gathered up from the floor a handful of the sketches which he had ripped out of his notebook, and put them under a book on the table, away from the housekeeper's prying eyes.

Dr. Grantling had been right. This morning every muscle hurt and the big bruise on her hip was acutely painful.

On the table in the living room there was a sealed note marked: "Kay."

"Good morning! Max is sending the coffee jar for a fingerprint check. Plans will go ahead as we discussed them. I am enclosing a key for the Pontiac. Try, if possible, to keep Nelly out of the house between one and two. No visitors last night. I love you." It was signed with the somewhat stylized initials D.R. that appeared on all his pictures.

After a long hot bath, which alleviated some of her discomfort, Kay dressed and hung the sling around her neck. Her hand was still swollen and the wrist ached. In the kitchen she turned her back so Mrs. Brundle could pull up the zipper on her dress.

"You look some better," the housekeeper said, "but you're no credit to my cooking and that's a fact. I'm fixing you a real nice omelet and some croissants I baked yesterday. I found some strawberries in the market and I got heavy cream to go with them. Expensive as sin, of course, but you need fattening up. And it's time someone used all the Forbes money." Her jaw dropped. "Honestly, I forgot, Kay, that it's gone."

Kay, on the verge of telling her that the money was safe, checked her indiscretion. "I can still eat," she assured the chagrined woman, "and it would be a mortal sin to waste your cooking on poor ingredients."

Mrs. Brundle deftly folded the fluffy golden brown omelet and put the plate in front of Kay. "You know what, people are beginning to talk about my cooking. Mrs. Weeks called and asked me to help her this afternoon. Once a year she gives a big tea and I'm to prepare the cakes and salads and sandwiches."

"Have you ever thought of starting a catering service? Preparing meals for people who can't cook or who want something special, and then delivering them hot at dinnertime?"

"That's an idea."

"Oh, by the way, Mr. Ransom is lending me his car this afternoon and I thought perhaps Nelly would like to go for a drive."

"She'd love it. She don't get out much. I don't know why people sort of neglect her."

"Then I'll call her as soon as I've finished breakfast."

"Mr. Ransom's car," Mrs. Brundle said, her

curiosity awakened. "He's sure being friendly."

"These croissants are simply wonderful. I've never eaten better ones."

"I've seen that man of his around the village a lot. How he gets his work done, I can't imagine."

"I don't suppose there's much to do at the studio."

"He's always using that public telephone booth on the Green when there's a perfectly good phone in the studio. Makes you wonder what he's got to say that he's afraid of people hearing."

"The people in this village wonder about everything."

"No harm in it that I can see when there's nothing to hide. I haven't heard that dog this morning. He usually makes a frightful rumpus when I drive up."

Kay pushed back her chair. "I'll call Nelly now."

Nelly, as might be expected, accepted promptly. "Mr. Ransom's car! My, that will be a thrill. I don't suppose he'd be going along."

"I imagine he's busy painting. After all, that's what he's here for."

"Oh, well, at least it's something to tell people, that I rode in Deke Ransom's own car. Did you get me his autograph?"

"Not yet." Kay remembered guiltily that she had forgotten to ask.

"I thought as you're right next door, you'd be seeing quite a lot of him."

For a wild moment Kay wondered whether

Nelly knew that Deke had spent the night in her house.

That morning there were no signs of life from the studio. Presumably Deke and Max were sleeping late to make up for their night's vigil and Wilma was waking reluctantly to face another empty day.

"Did you ever find out if that girl at Ransom's takes drugs?" Mrs. Brundle asked.

"I'd better spend the morning going over my clothes. I need to weed things out and see what I have ready for spring."

"Anything you don't need," Mrs. Brundle suggested, "I could make over for Nelly. You've got a real flair for clothes, Kay. Always did have. Not exactly fancy, but always looking just right, somehow."

Promptly at a quarter of one Kay left the house. A few minutes earlier she had seen Deke and Max stroll past and start down the incline.

It wasn't until she turned the key in the ignition of the Pontiac that she remembered what they had all forgotten, that she had one arm in a sling. For a moment she was flooded with such relief at having a legitimate excuse for not driving that she nearly laughed aloud. Then she recalled that Deke and Max were counting on her to have the Brundle house empty so they could examine Dan's belongings; that is, if they were Dan's. She removed the sling, tossed it into the back seat, and started the motor. With automatic transmission and power steering it was, she discovered, possible to control the car with one hand, but she would have to drive slowly and be careful on turns.

In a way, the pain caused by holding the wheel with her left hand was so immediate that it overrode her fear of driving. Or rather the fear was of a different kind; it was a real situation she had to face, not an imaginary one.

She went over the incline, down the road, across the ravine, and then had to use both hands to make the sharp turn onto the main road. For a moment she was sick with pain, but as it subsided she was flooded with a sense of triumph. She hadn't been afraid!

Someone waved to her and she recognized Worth on his way to work.

One part of Deke's plan had puzzled her, how he and Max expected to get into the Brundle house unseen by neighbors, but as she drew up at the door she realized that there was slight risk of their being noticed. For a man in Dan Ransom's job, a man who wanted his comings and goings to be as inconspicuous as possible, the location had been ideal. The Brundles lived in the only house on this narrow lane that was occupied during the cold weather, and their lodger's room, behind the living room on the first floor, had a private entrance.

Nelly, wearing a new spring coat of a violent green that made her face look yellow, had evidently been on the lookout, for she opened the door as soon as the car stopped and came to climb in beside Kay.

"Where would you like to go?" Kay asked politely.

"I was just thinking you haven't been to the cemetery yet. I heard someone speaking of it just the other day. You know how people talk." Nelly's eyes slid over Kay's face. "Would you like to go there now?"

"Not today."

Nelly's tongue licked out over her lips, rather like a snake's. "Ma says you were planning to marry Mr. Billings." Kay, trying to negotiate a corner without putting too much pressure on her lame wrist, made no comment. "Real good-looking, Ma said, "and a pleasant way with him."

Kay had turned onto a winding road, driving slowly, her eyes on the blue line of distant hills. Low stone fences made patterns in the fields.

"Of course," Nelly went on, "no one blames you for what happened. Ma said that road was a caution. But it must have been awful when it happened. Ma said that when she looked at that burned-out Cadillac, at what — was left —"

"Don't," Kay choked. "Please don't speak of it."

"Well, I'm sure I'm sorry if I hurt you." Nelly was offended. "How long does Mr. Ransom plan to stay?"

"I really don't know."

"Ma says you and he hit it off right away."

"The Hammonds asked us both to dinner," Kay said.

"Those rich friends of yours. I heard they'd come back unexpectedly. No one knows why. They don't usually honor us until the weather is nice. But it's good for business, of course, having them here. You should hear the orders to the butcher! Crown roasts and I don't know what all. And from the liquor store they got a case of some special claret, that's a kind of wine, to drink with their supper at night. I guess they'll make us feel pretty small-town, the way we live, after their foreign ways. Though I always say America's good enough for me."

Kay braked as a stray kitten crossed the road, taking its time.

"She was Sylvia Forrest. I can remember her coming up here when she was just a kid with braces on her teeth." Nelly added thoughtfully, "I've always had good teeth, I'm thankful to say."

The better to eat you with, my dear, Kay thought. Her left wrist was beginning to throb and she moved her hand on the wheel. Nelly noticed the swollen fingers, the strapped wrist.

"Ma said you took a fall, tripped on the stairs in the night. I knew Dr. Grantling was called. Mrs. Grantling was telling someone Doctor had to see you again. She said Mr. Ransom had called about you. Quite late at night, she said."

Kay made no comment. She remembered a trick she had used as a child when she wanted to make time pass in a hurry, dragging time like Christmas Eve, when she had to wait for morning to know what was under the tree. She began to write poetry to herself.

"They never did get an X-ray of your head, did they?" The tip of Nelly's nose twitched.

That's my last duchess painted on the wall,
Looking as if she were alive. I call
That piece a wonder, now.

"The Hammonds have company, I guess, judging by the amount of food they order. You'd think they would have a private phone," Nelly said in a tone of criticism. "But they're on a party line just like almost everyone else. They can afford to have everything."

"Right now what the Hammonds have is three cases of chicken pox to take care of."

"Well, you don't say!" Nelly always brightened at the disasters of others. "I wonder why no one told me about that."

"Why should they?" Kay's control of her tongue was slipping. A whole hour of this, she thought in a sudden rage against Deke. By that time Dr. Grantling would probably have to put her in Fenwick. In fact, she'd actually prefer Fenwick. Any place without Nelly would be a haven.

"Why, Kay, I hope you don't think I'm being nosy. But I'm not like you and Sylvia Hammond. I take an interest in the village. I like people. Sylvia never even noticed I was alive. She took up with that piano player, though he didn't have a cent to bless himself with. Now he seems to be spending a lot, though no one knows where he gets it. The wife of one of the bank officials says she knows for a fact that he doesn't get it from Sylvia."

A crow rose drunkenly from beside a dead raccoon and moved away as the car advanced.

"People are certainly funny," Nelly said as though she had discovered a new law of the universe. "Take Percy Willis now, that nice photographer who stayed with us. Percy's kind of a distinguished name, I think. But he never answered a question, just turned everything into a kind of joke so you didn't know where you were with him or even if he was laughing at you. He never even once asked me to look at the pictures he took or anything. What do you do with a man like that?"

"Ignore him," Kay advised her.

"You can't hardly do that when he's practically a guest in your own house and you want to make things nice for him, make him feel at home."

"If your mother's cooking couldn't do that, nothing could." Kay switched abruptly to her suggestion that Mrs. Brundle make a business of catering.

"It might work." Nelly was not enthusiastic. "Only thing is that it wouldn't bring anyone to the house and Ma likes having a lodger. It's nice to have a man in the house. That's why we are hoping Mr. Worth will stay on after his operation. I could look after him until he gets steady work of some kind in the village."

"How did he know you people take in lodgers?"

"Well," Nelly said simply, "with the motel closed until Decoration Day and the Wistons gone to Florida this year, there was no one else who takes lodgers. Not with board, too. Where could he of gone?" She added with a smirk, "Sometimes I think it was meant."

Kay refused to rise to the bait. The time dragged endlessly. Though Nelly enjoyed riding in the Pontiac, particularly because it belonged to Deke Ransom, and she was eager to have everyone see her — she waved extravagantly at every acquaintance she saw on the street — she was thwarted in her insistent search for information about Ernest Billings, about Deke Ransom, about the disappearance of Kay's money, and that queer story she had told of murder. She was insatiable in her curiosity about the private lives of the Hammonds.

"Charlie Hammond married Sylvia for her money, of course. Anyone could see that."

"They are more in love than any couple I know," Kay retorted. "That's a vicious thing to say, Nelly."

"Well, I'm sure! I think you get queerer every day, Kay. I make a harmless comment —"

"What's so harmless about it?"

After that the drive was a hopeless failure. Even when Kay looked at a village clock and saw that only three-quarters of an hour had passed, she gave up and drove Nelly home.

They exchanged artificial smiles.

"It was a lovely ride, Kay."

"I enjoyed it."

Having rid herself, of her unwelcome passenger, Kay was belatedly aware of the harm she might have done. She waited anxiously in the car until Nelly had gone inside, until she could see her at an upstairs window, looking out in surprise at the motionless Pontiac. Then she released the brake, relieved to know that Deke and Max had already left the house and presumably without leaving any evidence to betray their presence.

She had crossed the bridge over the ravine and started up the hill when she saw the man ahead of her, walking at an easy pace, hands in his pockets, head lowered as though deep in somber thought. She touched the horn and drew up beside him.

Deke turned and as she moved over in the seat, he slid under the wheel. He looked at her in dismay.

"I ought to be shot! I forgot about your sprained wrist. It must hurt like hell."

"It does. What I want to know is whether it was worth it."

"We got in without any difficulty and found the stuff in the attic. Some of it I identified as Dan's, a favorite old sweater, things like that. The photographic equipment, of course, was camouflage he had acquired somewhere. Max lifted some fingerprints and he's shooting the stuff through to headquarters now, but we're sure of what we believed before: Mrs. Brundle's missing lodger was Dan."

After a look at his face Kay was silent.

"He was five years younger than I," Deke said at last, "and about five times as bright. You'd have liked him, I think, Kay. There was so much ahead for him and only five months of marriage. They were so much in love it made you feel good just to see them together."

He stopped the car, reached back for the discarded sling, adjusted it for Kay. For a moment they sat without speaking. Then he said, "We've both had a rough time, and if you can forgive me for persuading you to drive with that sprained wrist, it's more than I can forgive myself."

"It really didn't hurt all that much, and it was worth it, Deke. I won't be afraid to drive again. I'm cured."

"On the kill-or-cure principle."

"Self-flagellation," she mocked him.

He laughed with her. "So it is. Come over to the studio and we'll have a drink to celebrate."

"Celebrate what?"

"Freedom from fear," he told her and helped her out of the car.

Worth was inspecting a patch of ground as they walked toward him. "That's crab grass, Miss Forbes," he said in a tone of consternation. "We ought to get rid of it before it takes over. I finished mowing the front of the place and I'll clear away the grass and weeds before I start in back."

Concerned by his patent fatigue, Kay said, "That's enough for today. The place looks better already."

"Well, if it suits you," he said reluctantly. "I haven't put in more'n an hour this afternoon."

"Go ahead if you feel up to it." Kay had remembered that the wages were important to him.

He brightened. "I could do at least another hour's work."

"And maybe Mr. Ransom will have some odd jobs to do now and then," she suggested rashly.

Worth looked in surprise at Deke. "You the Mr. Ransom who rents the studio?"

"Yes. Why?"

"Well, I don't know. Only I thought I heard people talking over there, rather loud, as though they were quarreling. I thought you were home."

"There's no one there except — come on, Kay." Deke quickened his pace toward the studio.

There was no one in the big studio room, nothing had been altered. Deke called, "Wilma?" When there was no answer, he called again. Then he ran up the stairs, tapped on the door, and finally opened it.

He raced down the stairs, passed Kay without seeming to be aware of her presence, flung open the door of the storeroom.

In the first moment after he found the light,

Kay saw all that mattered: there was another dead rat in the trap; Wilma lay sprawled on the floor, the back of her head matted with blood; and scattered over her, over the floor, over boxes and packages and pieces of furniture, were pieces of crumpled newspaper. Tossed on top of rusted bedsprings were the two red and white striped canvas carry-alls. They were empty.

CHAPTER 16

Wilma Ransom, lying in the big bed in Paul
Forbes's room, still dazed, tried to answer Dr.
Grantling's questions. They had been lucky in
catching him as he was leaving the Hammond
house. She had been taking a nap and was awakened by the sound of footsteps downstairs. Not
loud footsteps, she explained; she would have
assumed either Deke or Max was there. These
had been cautious footsteps; and then she had
heard something being moved in the storeroom
and the rustle of paper.

She had gone downstairs and found the door
of the storeroom open, but she had stumbled on
the stairs and alerted the housebreaker. The light
had been on but she had seen no one. Probably
he had been hiding behind the open door, but
she had caught sight of the dead rat in the trap
and had cried out. That was all she remembered.

"You've been taking some kind of barbiturate,
haven't you?" Dr. Grantling asked. He had
cleaned and bandaged her head. There was nothing seriously wrong.

"Seconal. I hadn't been sleeping. My husband
— died suddenly a few weeks ago. The sleeping
pills were my physician's suggestion. I'll give you
his name if you like. He warned me that he

wouldn't refill the prescription. I'm not an addict."

Standing beside the bed, Dr. Grantling said, "There's something wrong about this place. I think this incident should be reported to the police."

"It has been," Kay said tartly. "You don't think we'd let her be hurt and not do anything about it, do you? And you're not sending her to Fenwick, Doctor, because someone hit her on the head."

The doctor looked from Wilma's shadowed eyes to Kay's challenging ones. He shrugged. "Have it your own way, but I can tell you one thing, Miss Forbes; I wouldn't want a daughter of mine staying in this place unless she had a couple of strong men to guard her."

"I will have," Kay assured him. As he picked up his bag, she added, "I hope no one needs to hear of this, Doctor. There's been enough gossip."

"I am not a gossip," the doctor said stiffly.

"But as I have reason to know, your home phone is on a party line."

"I'll be silent as the grave," he promised, seemed to listen to his own words and regret them.

Deke was waiting in the living room when Kay accompanied the doctor to the door. The latter took a long, speculative look at him, another at Kay.

"Well," he said heavily, "you're of age, but I

hope you know what you are doing, Miss Forbes."

As he went out, Max was coming across the lawn and Kay waited for him.

"Is Ransom here?"

"Yes, come in, Mr. — uh, I don't really know your last name."

"Max will do." He followed her into the living room where Deke told him quickly what they had found in the storeroom.

"Wilma wasn't badly hurt, just a glancing blow that bled a lot and knocked her out. Kay is going to look after her."

"Turn and turn about is fair play," Kay said.

Max raised his brows and Deke nodded.

"I've told Kay all about the setup." Observing Max's unconcealed disapproval, he expostulated, "My God, you have to trust someone!"

"Not in my job," Max said briefly.

"Considering what's been done to those two girls, I can't say much for your methods." Deke was angry.

Max, now that he had been restored to his own position, dropped wearily into a chair. "I'm sorry about Wilma. Tell me all over again, Miss Forbes, just what happened when you and Ransom got home. Take your time. I want details."

Kay told him of Worth's surprise at hearing Ransom had not been home, of the sounds of a quarrel, the search for Wilma, and the discovery of the empty canvas carry-alls. Deke had carried Wilma over to the house, they had caught the doctor as he was going by, and Wilma had said she had been struck down without seeing who hit her.

Max listened, pulling at his lower lip. He made her go over the whole story again.

"Well?" Deke asked at last.

"Okay, I slipped up," Max agreed. "I set a trap for my man and all we caught was a rat. The wrong rat. I shouldn't have let you go along. If you had stayed at the studio, no one would have got in and Wilma wouldn't have been attacked."

"I identified Dan's sweater and those neckties. You couldn't have done that."

"Yeah, but I got his fingerprints. They were all I needed to prove he'd been there."

"You haven't had a report on them yet," Deke reminded him.

Max shrugged.

"You're holding out," Deke said at last. "You've got something."

Max gave Kay a doubtful look.

"I'm involved in this, too," she reminded him.

"I got a report on that jar of instant coffee," Max said reluctantly.

Deke brandished a book with a threatening gesture and Max laughed. "Okay. The prints were on file. Belong to a guy named Wayne Graham who was released from Sing Sing just four months ago. Jewel thief. He had pulled only a few jobs, but they were big ones, same *modus operandi*. Some of the stuff was recovered. The rest he had already sold. The money he realized on the jewelry has never been unearthed and no one ever located the fence he used."

"Ernest?" Kay asked at last.

"Don't know yet. I've sent on that cuff link on the off chance it ties in with one of the robberies — and then — other things —"

When Deke found Max had nothing more to volunteer, he said heavily, "So we walked out and he walked in. He knows the Forbes money is out of his reach. We've lost him. There's nothing now to bring him back."

"There's Miss Forbes who knows what he looks like."

"Then you think he'll try again?"

"I think," Max said coolly, "he'll have to try again."

"Then he's still around somewhere," Kay said shakily.

"I think I know now where he is," Max said.

"How did you find out?" Deke demanded.

"Miss Forbes told me." Max got up. "I'm going back to the studio. They'll be calling me any time and that's the only number they have. I assume you'll be staying here, Ransom."

"I'll be here."

There was a small silence in the room after he had gone. Kay went up to look at Wilma, who was sleeping quietly.

When she returned, Deke asked, "All right?"

"I think so. She's asleep. She doesn't seem to be in any pain."

"There's one thing that bothers me," Deke

said. "I don't see this fellow, whoever he is, being so damned omniscient unless he has an accomplice somewhere. Kay, how well do you know the Hammonds?"

"They're my best friends."

"I said — know them."

She met his eyes and said, "I don't believe it. I absolutely refuse. Not Charlie Hammond. Aside from the fact that he couldn't conceivably be the accomplice of a jewel thief, he doesn't need the money. Sylvia inherited all the Forrest money, millions of it."

"Nice to have, of course, but she's nobody's fool. A girl with that background learns young to keep an eye out for fortune hunters. He'd need something of his own to keep his end up."

"No," Kay said.

Deke got up to answer the tap at the door. Max did not come in. "I'm taking the Pontiac. Just had a call and I don't dare take it on a party line. I'll be back in half an hour. Are you armed?"

"I can take care of myself and the two girls a hell of a lot better than you have," Deke said impatiently.

"We're closing in. This time it's for keeps."

"All right, grandmother."

Max nodded without smiling and went out. The car door slammed. A moment later the Pontiac rolled past the house. As he reached the incline, Max tapped the horn lightly.

"I'd better do something about planning dinner, if I've got to feed all three of you." Kay

217

laughed when Deke insisted on accompanying her to the kitchen.

"I don't intend to let you out of my sight," he declared.

Mrs. Brundle had prepared a chicken and mushroom casserole. Fortunately she always cooked far larger quantities than Kay could conceivably eat. She checked on materials for a salad and found a can of asparagus.

"At least we won't starve," she said cheerfully.

"We've been living on ham and eggs and canned stuff, over at the studio, because Wilma can't cook."

The call from the State Police Barracks came a few minutes later. The police had, they said, tried to reach Mr. Ransom at the studio and then had called the Forbes house. They wanted him to come at once. They had picked up a man whom they believed to be the prowler about whom Mr. Ransom had reported.

"I'll make it in an hour," Deke said.

There was a sharp exchange of words. Then Deke said, "All right, but I'll have to walk down. My car isn't here. It will take me about a quarter of an hour."

He hung up. "They sit on their hands for three weeks and now they can't wait even a few minutes. I don't like leaving you, Kay, but it won't take long. They'll drive me back and Max should be here long before that."

Seeing his distress, she said reassuringly, "I'll lock up after you. Don't worry about me. And

I'll look after Wilma."

He took the small gun out of his pocket and held it out to her. Kay backed away.

"No, I don't want it. I'd be more afraid of using it than of anything else. I might hurt someone."

Deke gave a shout of laughter, held her tightly for a moment, and then was gone.

Kay locked and bolted the door and fastened the chain. Back in the living room she moved around restlessly. She picked up a book, tossed it aside unopened, and then saw the crumpled sketches Deke had made the night before. She smoothed them out and examined them. There were half a dozen of her, one of Mrs. Brundle squeezing under the wheel of the jeep; one of a girl with a laughing, sunlit face at which Kay stared in perplexity. There was something familiar about it. Then she realized, with a sense of shock, that the happy face belonged to Wilma, a Wilma she had never known. There was a sketch of Worth pushing the lawn mower, another of him walking across the lawn with a long free stride, flinging out an arm in a wide gesture.

Worth? She stared at the sketch, her heart beginning to race. Bald head, dark glasses, unsightly mouth. But — give him black hair, take away the glasses, the unsightly teeth, the pallor — no, she was imagining things. She must be.

But she wasn't. Prison pallor, she thought. That dark skin must have been a stain of some sort.

In a moment she got up and went to the

219

telephone. After a short pause she jiggled it impatiently. Even when she knew that it was dead, she did not react. She was waiting passively. "This time," Max had said, "we are playing for keeps." Her luck had run out.

Almost without surprise she saw Ernest standing in the doorway. He had pulled off the dark glasses. He stood looking at her, rubbing the stain from his teeth.

She heard herself saying, incredibly, "Baldness isn't becoming to you."

"You have to sacrifice something," he said in his familiar, resonant voice. "It hurts me more than it does you but it will grow back." He added, "Where is it, Kay?"

"You don't think I'd tell you?"

"Yes, I think you would." He sounded amused.

"Deke and Max are on their way over from the studio."

His white teeth flashed as he smiled. "They are both away and they aren't coming back. What have you done with the money?"

"The man who has been posing as Mr. Ransom's servant is a Treasury agent, Ernest. Mr. Ransom is the older brother of the Treasury man you killed. Wilma is his widow. Max has identified your fingerprints on the jar of instant coffee as those of Wayne Graham, a jewel thief."

"Where is the money?" Ernest Billings — or Worth — or Wayne Graham — repeated.

"Max put it in the local bank."

"How do you know?"

"I have the receipt."

"Then," Ernest said, "we'll have to go get it. Start moving, Kay. If the law knows about me, there's no time to waste."

"I won't. You can't make me."

He laughed, the joyous, infectious laughter she had loved, and there was a switchblade in his hand, pressing against her side. As she stood unmoving, the knife slid through her dress, scratched her skin. Watching her, he laughed again.

"Where's your coat?"

She walked past him like an automaton, taking out her lipstick, which seemed to strike him as irresistibly funny. For a moment she leaned against the table, then she walked out of the room, head high.

He followed her to the hall closet, pulled the coat over her shoulders, steered her to the door, holding her arm in a firm grip.

Hidden in bushes, halfway down the incline, was a Mercury. He held the right-hand door for her, the switchblade in his hand. When she was inside, he went around to the driver's seat. She watched while he adjusted a rough brown toupee to cover the part of his head he had shaved and that matched the dye job; he carefully attached a small mustache and put on steel-rimmed glasses.

Seeing her expression, he laughed again. "The trick isn't so much in the physical changes, it's in the kind of person you decide to be." His manner was that of a somewhat diffident and prim schoolteacher.

"You'll have to do something about that prison pallor," she said gently. "It spoils the image." Then she realized that he was a dangerous man to laugh at. Mockery would be the one weapon to which his kind of vanity was vulnerable.

"Now I'll tell you how we're going to handle this," he said. "It is now a quarter of three. We'll reach the bank just before the doors close and you'll give them a receipt and ask for the stuff that was deposited for you. No tricks. No signals. If you raise a single doubt, I'll have nothing to lose. In that case I'm taking you with me, Kay. From the beginning it's been one damned frustrating thing after another: first this T man gets in the way, then those watchdogs guarded the place at night, then —"

"Then," Kay said quietly, "I didn't go under the subway train or break my neck on the stairs or drink the instant coffee. How does it feel, Ernest, to stab a woman in the back? Challenging? Exciting? Heroic?"

"The hell of it is that I'll probably never meet another woman I'll be so crazy about. I knew from the beginning you were a calculated risk. You and your standards. And yet you got under my skin. It seemed worth it at the time."

The car moved down the incline. If Ernest remembered that he had killed a man there, that Uncle Paul had died of fright, that she had been knocked unconscious, there was no indication of it in his good-looking face.

"Ernest, Wayne, whatever your name is, why did you become a criminal? With your intelligence and ability and charm you could have succeeded in almost any field you attempted."

"Criminal? Well, maybe I am from your point of view. Right and wrong are all nice and clear-cut to you, aren't they? Everything is black or white."

"I'm not that much of a fool. But why do you object to the name when you don't object to the thing itself?"

"Darling Kay, must you be so self-righteous? Show me a big businessman or industrialist or top-flight lawyer and I'll show you what you would call a criminal who just hasn't been found out. The survival of the fittest."

The Mercury turned onto the side road. Kay looked in both directions, hoping to see a patrol car, but there was nothing on the road except for an oil truck a quarter of a mile away.

"So I was mistaken about you," she said calmly.

"You were in love with me. You are still in love with me. Perhaps, after all, I have the qualities you want and you just don't know it."

"I mean I was mistaken about your intelligence," Kay said, still in a detached tone as though discussing a stranger. "You think the world is a jungle. You think you can simply take what you want. And I doubt your ability, too, or you wouldn't have spent years in Sing Sing when brighter men were free to live as they chose."

He was driving with his left hand, his right on the seat between them grasping the switchblade. His knuckles whitened as his fingers closed hard on the knife. He hadn't liked that. He hadn't liked it at all. But she wasn't going to die with a whimper, she told herself. She wasn't going to throw in the towel.

"And you don't have any of the qualities I want," she went on. "If there's anything less attractive than a juvenile delinquent, it's an adult delinquent. I like a man whose honor I can rely on."

"Like Ransom," he said between his teeth. "You really fell for him."

"I really did," she admitted.

"The big shot who plays it safe," he said. "The stuffed shirt. So I take risks. So I'm a one-time loser. That won't happen again. Anyhow, who the hell wants to be safe? I like challenges. I like excitement. And when four hundred thousand bucks fall into my lap — and you were going to declare it, pay out God knows how much to Uncle Sam —"

"Just how much do you think you are going to pay to Uncle Sam?" she asked quietly. "All the rest of your life."

"He has to get me first," Ernest pointed out.

"You thought fast, didn't you? While you were clearing the snow off Uncle Paul's car, you put the brakes out of commission."

"You can believe me or not, Kay, I didn't want to do it but you and your uncle were the only people who knew about those canvas bags."

"And you were determined to have them."

"I am still determined to have them. Why, on that money I could live in comfort for the rest of my life, have every luxury I want."

"What you want most," she reminded him, "in the way of luxury is space, freedom, and privacy. Even the best prisons don't provide them, Ernest."

The village Green was almost deserted. There were cars parked in the circular driveway in front of Dr. Grantling's square white house. A couple of women had stopped to gossip outside the drugstore. Ernest pulled into a parking space in front of the bank.

"Okay, this is it, Kay. Just one false move and you'll have had it."

He assisted her from the car, walked close beside her, the point of the switchblade, concealed by the sleeve of his overcoat, against her side.

A couple of tellers were talking in their cages. At one of the officer's desks near the window a man was arranging a loan. At the other the executive was putting away papers. He looked up at Kay.

"I am Kay Forbes."

The executive got to his feet. "Glad to meet you, Miss Forbes. We were sorry to hear of your uncle's death. A great loss to the community. A great loss. What can I do for you?"

"A friend of mine deposited some packages for me for safekeeping. I would like to have them now, please."

He looked from her steady eyes to the quiet man who stood so close beside her.

In a few minutes the bank doors closed for the day, shades were drawn down, but the tellers continued to work. Somewhere an adding machine clattered rapidly, paper was jerked out of a typewriter. Ernest made no movement, but Kay was aware of his growing tension.

Then the official was back, gently apologetic for the delay, asking Kay to sign for the four large packages which a couple of clerks were carrying.

For a moment she thought of changing her signature to alert him then, as the knife scratched her side, she signed hastily.

With a little ejaculation of concern over her arm in its sling, the official insisted that his clerks carry the packages to the car.

Ernest helped Kay into the Mercury and got behind the wheel. He was smiling to himself. Half turning in the seat, Kay saw one of the clerks look at the license number on the car; then he went back to the bank at a run. She smiled too.

CHAPTER 17

Outside the village the car picked up speed though the man who had called himself Ernest Billings was careful not to drive too fast. Speeders in Connecticut lose their driving licenses, and there were some chances he did not want to take, not with those bundles of currency on the back seat.

Kay, feeling curiously calm, sat trying to find a way out. Her chief hope was that the bank official's suspicions had been aroused. His clerk had taken the license number of the car. Surely he would report to the police. At any moment a patrol car would follow them, or there would be road blocks ahead.

That possibility drew dimmer as twilight began to fall. Ernest was avoiding toll roads, sticking to minor secondary roads where the possibility of encountering police cars was remote.

"You can't get away with it," she said at last.

"I did get away with it. I've got the money and I've got you."

"How do you intend to dispose of me?"

There was a long pause before he said, "Kay, if you were a different kind of girl, if you could just forget those damned standards of yours, we could have a wonderful time. I've never been so crazy about a girl. I could show you more life, more thrills, than you've ever dreamed of. We could go to Brazil and live high on the hog."

"Brazil has signed an extradition treaty with this country."

"Then somewhere else." He was impatient. "How about it? We're headed for a terrific future if you'll say the word."

He really seemed to think that she believed him, that she would consider his fantastic proposition.

"You're headed for prison, Ernest, and this time it's for life. Nothing alters that." She added sharply, "Where are you going?"

He had turned into a village, stopped before a public telephone booth.

"You are going to call the Hammonds and you are going to make it good, Baby. Someone noticed this license plate at the bank." He laughed as he saw her chagrin. "Did you think I didn't see that? We're going to take the police off our track. You are going to say that you are about crazy, that you can't stay there any longer, remembering poor Ernest. You're going to say not to worry, that you have plenty of money, and you'll be in touch."

"You really are a devil!"

He laughed. "If anyone gets any ideas, that will take care of them. But no double talk. I'll be right beside you."

He crowded into the booth with her, dropped

coins and dialed the number, then handed the phone to Kay.

It was Charlie Hammond who answered. "Kay! Where the hell are you? Ransom just called and he's nearly out of his mind. He got a fake telephone message —"

Kay laughed. "I know. You never can be sure about them, can you?" When Charlie was silent, she repeated, "Can you? And that's really why I am calling you now. I'm going away, Charlie. I've got to. Simply got to. Because of Ernest. I wasn't able to stay in that house one more minute. But tell Sylvia not to worry. I have plenty of money and I'll get in touch — when I can."

"Just how free are you to talk?" Charlie asked quietly.

"Oh, not at all!" she assured him gaily. "Sometimes I think you and Sylvia are right about my mental condition. I just — had to get away. I knew you'd understand."

"Are you in danger?"

"Of course."

"God! Can you leave the receiver off?"

"I'll try. I'll call you in a few days." As Ernest stirred impatiently beside her, she said, "Goodby."

Ernest took the phone out of her hand and placed it back on the hook. "That's my girl. If you'd play along with me, Kay, we could have some good times. But if you try to get smart —" The point of the knife scraped her skin again.

Back in the Mercury he drove slowly, looking

at the parked cars. Abruptly he braked and pulled in at the curb, switching off lights.

Ahead there were two cars, each with a young couple in it, calling back and forth. Then someone said, "All right, it's more fun to go together."

One couple left their car and piled into the other. When the second car had moved on, Ernest slid out, opened the hood of the abandoned Ford and tinkered for a moment. Then he started the motor and came back to move the packages of money out of the Mercury. From inside the luggage compartment he pulled two JUST MARRIED signs and hung them over the license plates of the Ford.

"Come on," he told Kay, took her arm, forced her into the Ford.

In a few minutes he had headed toward a turnpike and was speeding south.

"Just in case someone got an idea at the bank about that Mercury," he told her gleefully.

"I believe you are enjoying this!"

"Don't you think it's exciting?" he asked.

"Excitement. That's an odd word for an adult. It sounds like a child's response to a circus."

He didn't like that.

"The owners of this Ford will report that it has been stolen."

"They're out for the evening. And who is going to be looking for a bride and groom?"

Kay made no comment. When he had changed cars, her hope dwindled of their being found. She had made her point to Charlie Hammond, he was sure she was aware that she had been forced away, but what good would it do? Deke had been drawn off by a fake call. He would know what had happened, but how could he find her? And Max? Max had said, "I know where he is; Miss Forbes told me."

But what had she said? Oh, of course, he had spotted the discrepancy. Ernest, as Worth, had said he heard angry voices, a quarrel, in the studio, but Wilma had heard nothing but footsteps. Max had guessed then that Worth was the man they were seeking. But he had had to get proof before he could make an arrest. Anyhow, if he were hunting for Worth, he'd never recognize Ernest as he was now.

"Why didn't you get away at once when you discovered that the money was gone?" she asked.

"I expected to find it." Ernest did not look at her. "And then there was some unfinished business."

"Me?"

"You."

"How did you get in the house?"

"I had a copy of Mrs. Brundle's key made several days ago and I came in while you and Ransom were looking after the girl."

"She had been married only five months to that Treasury agent you killed and she loved him."

Ernest made no comment.

They were going fast now, Ernest keeping the car at seventy miles an hour. Then, as the Saw-

231

mill Parkway is well patrolled, he slowed to fifty-five.

"What are you going to do to me, Ernest?"

"That depends on you, doesn't it?"

She couldn't open the car door and jump. Not at that speed. She couldn't run fast enough to get away from him anyhow. She could at least scream if she passed a police car. She began to roll down the window.

"Put it up, Kay."

"I feel faint. I need the air."

"Put it up or you'll feel worse." The switch-blade was in his hand again, it slid through the coat, scratched her side, pressed suddenly. She cried out as she felt blood trickle down her side.

She had nothing but her lipstick, which had so amused Ernest. She groped inside her handbag, opened a tiny address book that bore her name, scrawled "Help!" across the first page.

Out of the darkness came the lights of Yonkers. They were very close to New York now. The glow of the city lighted the sky.

Unexpectedly the directional lights blinked and he made a right-hand turn, pulled up at a small building marked "Motel Office."

For a moment he sat at the wheel pondering. Then he pulled off the sling and forced her arm into the coat. "You're coming along and I don't want them to think I beat you into submission. Not a word or a sign, Kay. I mean that."

Side by side they entered the office. The clerk, glancing out at the car, at the sign "Just Married," grinned at them.

Ernest registered for Mr. and Mrs. Herbert Wilson, and the clerk handed him a key.

"Number Fourteen. Nice and comfortable. Private. The end of the row. Good luck to you both."

Ernest laughed. "Thanks for your good wishes."

"There's a nice restaurant here. Maybe," the manager chuckled, "you'd rather have food sent in."

"That's an idea. I'll call from the room."

"It closes at nine-thirty. You'll have to order by nine."

Standing at the office door, the manager grinned as he saw the solicitous manner in which Ernest assisted his bride into the car. A small dark object dropped on the ground.

When Ernest had unlocked the door and switched on the lights in the room, he said, "All right, go in."

"No," Kay said "I won't." She took a long breath. Before she could scream, he lifted her and carried her over the threshold. She could hear the manager laugh. She turned her head, saw him bend to pick up the address book. A gust of wind blew it away.

At the police barracks a patient lieutenant was trying to cope with Deke Ransom, Max, a bank official and the Hammonds, who had arrived in a state bordering on frenzy. To add to the confusion, reports kept coming in for Max.

The lieutenant found himself on the defensive. He had goofed in assuming that the accident in which Paul Forbes and Dan Ransom had been killed was what it purported to be. Now he was in a mess. A Treasury agent had been murdered and buried under a false name. Kay Forbes had been kidnaped along with a fortune in currency.

The worst of it was that, from the beginning, he had openly discredited the girl's story. It had sounded fantastic and everyone knew — he corrected himself — everyone had believed that she was mentally unstable. Even the doctor had thought she was a mental case, he defended himself, but he was not happy.

A jittery bank official had called the barracks and said there had been something queer about the girl when she came in for the package which a Treasury agent had left in her name the day before. His description of the quiet man with her didn't fit anyone in the case. The official had insisted on coming along to the barracks. If he had made a mistake, four hundred thousand dollars had been lost through his bad judgment.

Deke Ransom was not only the brother of the dead Treasury agent; he was also one of America's most famous and respected writers. No one had ever challenged the soundness of his facts nor the fairness of his judgment. What he could do to the State Police, in one of his widely syndicated articles, made the lieutenant blanch.

The Hammonds represented the most powerful money force in the community, though it was true, the harrassed lieutenant conceded, that they had never used money for power. They weren't attempting to do it even now.

"It was the timing, of course," Max said. "I went down to the telephone booth on the Green to take that call. Wayne Graham, or whatever his name is, had been hanging around as Worth. He went to the studio, made a fake call to Ransom, and then took the girl away."

"Do you suppose she knows who he is by now?" Deke asked.

"You made a sketch of Worth and she left it on the table. She'd made an exclamation mark on it with a lipstick." Max put the sketch on the table. "Of course the chances are that he doesn't look like that now, but it's some kind of guide."

"All that I could make out," the bank official said, "was that she looked sort of strained. And taking the packages that way. And she didn't sit down while she waited. Just stood beside that man. That's why I had my clerk get the license number of the Mercury he was driving."

"Did the man look like this?" Max handed him the sketch of Worth.

"Not at all. He wasn't bald, he had sort of rough brown hair, a small mustache, steel-rimmed glasses. Very respectable-looking, a little prim. Might be a teacher. He was just so — still. That was what made me notice him. And he stood so close to the girl."

Deke sketched rapidly. "More like that?"

"Yes, except his expression was more — uh — it was firmer."

"We'll get that on the wires," the lieutenant said.

"I knew as soon as she telephoned that something was wrong," Charlie said. "I think he must have been right beside her. And she gave me all the hints she could, about the fact that the call might be a fake, that she had to go because of Ernest —"

"She said that?" Deke interrupted.

"She did. And when I asked if she were in danger, she laughed and said she was. Then she capped it all by saying Sylvia and I had been right in telling her she was mentally off balance."

"As if we ever had," Sylvia said fiercely.

"Where in the name of God has he taken her?" Deke exclaimed.

The telephone rang and the lieutenant scooped it in.

"They've found the Mercury," he reported. "Small town about twenty miles north of here. Stole a Ford with a Connecticut license. We'll send out word not to look for the Mercury and get our men on the Ford."

"Heading north then," Max said.

"He's avoiding the toll roads. No trace of them anywhere."

The next call was for Max. The cuff link Kay had found was part of the Welman robbery, the one on which Wayne Graham had been convicted and for which he had spent three years in prison.

Reports kept coming in but they were all negative. No trace of the stolen Ford had been found. Deke's sketch was being distributed widely, but there was no assurance the man had not again changed his appearance. Front and profile pictures taken after Graham's conviction were also being sent out.

"He wouldn't hurt her," Sylvia said abruptly. "He couldn't hurt Kay."

"He's tried four times," Max said.

Deke said nothing at all. Sylvia's hand groped for Charlie's, clung to it.

The lieutenant sent for coffee and they drank it in silence, unbroken except for the constant coming and going of troopers, the ringing of the telephone. Each time there was a momentary surge of hope, then a descent into apathy.

"She wouldn't take my gun," Deke said. "She said she was afraid of hurting someone."

"They've got to stop for gas," Max pointed out.

"We're informing all service stations. We're reaching all the eating places we can but, my God, they can be anywhere in New England and there are thousands of places. Thousands."

"They'd have to sleep," Charlie said.

"A man can stay awake a long time if his freedom depends on it," the lieutenant told him.

"Well, I was just thinking of what I'd do if I were on the run."

The lieutenant laughed.

"You listen to Charlie," Sylvia snapped. "He's a lot smarter than anyone knows."

"I'm listening."

"Tonight the heat is on," Charlie said, "and there's not much traffic on the roads, especially not on those little New England roads he seems to be taking. Anyone stops him now and he's got a lot of explaining to do, and with a cop there Kay could — that is, if Kay still —" His voice faded, was strong again. "I'd hole up somewhere tonight and then in the morning I'd hit commuting traffic coming into a city, Hartford or New Haven or Boston, enough traffic so I wouldn't be noticed."

"You see?" Sylvia said triumphantly.

"Hole up where? Graham has always been a lone wolf. He hasn't worked with anyone. Miss Forbes is the only girl he's been interested in since his release. Hotels are out. Boarding houses are too intimate; he'd be remembered there."

"Motels?" Max suggested.

The lieutenant got on the phone again.

The next call was for Max. Ernest's luggage, which he had removed from the New York apartment, had been found in a Philadelphia waiting room marked, "Please Hold." There were three fingerprints under the handle of one of the suitcases. The fingerprints, like those in Worth's room at the Brundle house, were those of Wayne Graham.

"Philadelphia," Max said thoughtfully. "My

God! Because he started north there's no reason why he couldn't backtrack. He may be heading south."

As the lieutenant raised his telephone, Max warned him, "Be sure they don't scare the guy until they are ready to make the pinch. We've got to give that girl every chance we can."

"What chance do you think she has?" Deke asked. "He has the money. At this point she's a liability and he already has one murder on his record." He repeated, "What chance?"

CHAPTER 18

When Ernest had brought in the packages of money, he shoved them in the small closet. Then he straightened and walked slowly toward Kay. She backed away from him.

"What do you want?"

"What do you expect, darling Kay, on our wedding night?"

He meant it. She managed a smile. "There's only twenty minutes before the restaurant closes for the night. It's after nine and I am starving."

He gave her a long scrutinizing look and then he smiled back. He still believed that she was in love with him. Or perhaps he didn't care whether she was in love with him or not. She was there and she was his.

"I can't starve my bride," he said, called the restaurant and ordered dinner. As he reached out an arm to draw her toward him, Kay evaded him and went to the mirror to freshen her make-up.

"I must wash before I eat," she said casually.

Ernest shook his head. "Afraid not, darling. I'm not taking a chance on having you lock yourself in." He stood between her and the bath-room door, so close that she backed hastily away and sat down in an armchair. She refused a cigarette and massaged her painful left wrist.

240

Leaning against the table, Ernest smiled down at her. "You are my girl, you know. My lovely bride."

"I don't think I'd care much for a man who wanted to live on my money. You ought to try poor Nelly." Kay laughed.

That was a mistake. He was indifferent to her opinion of his ethics, but her contempt for him as a man was unbearable. He reached down and jerked her to her feet, into his arms, held her crushed against him, and bent his head to her mouth. An endless time seemed to pass before he lifted his head.

"Kay!" His face was deeply flushed and he was breathless, but his eyes were bright with triumph. "Kay!" He buried his face in her neck, one hand moving over her shoulders, down her back. Then he lifted her, carried her toward one of the twin beds.

"Please! Please!"

There was a tap at the door and he shoved his hand over her mouth taut, straining to hear.

"Room service," a voice called.

Kay pushed away his hand. "The wedding feast," she reminded him.

The switchblade appeared in his hand. "Come to the door with me. Not a sound."

The glitter in his eyes frightened her. The situation was out of her control. But, she vowed to herself, she would scream if it was the last thing she ever did; which, she was quite well aware, was more than possible.

Holding her against him, Ernest opened the door. A young man stood holding a heavy tray. Ernest fell back to let him in. The waiter eased the tray onto the table and turned, a revolver in his hand.

"All right, Graham. Let the girl go."

And then the room was filled with troopers and behind them came the manager, holding Kay's address book in his hand.

Ernest jerked Kay in front of him. "I have a switchblade against her back. Tell them, Kay. Feel it?"

She gasped, "Yes."

"Either we leave here together or she gets the whole length."

There was no movement in the room. Kay looked from face to face. Four troopers, guns drawn, stood helpless, afraid to risk her life. The manager watched, breathing fast with excitement. The knife suddenly pricked harder and Kay moaned.

Ernest took one step backward, drawing her with him toward the door. Then a second. The manager moved, flung the address book in Ernest's face, striking his eye. Ernest grunted and jerked his head. As he stumbled backward, Kay broke away and fell to her knees. A man flung himself on top of her. Over his protective body she saw Ernest turn the switchblade on himself and then drop it as a shot was fired.

"Got his arm," a trooper said coolly.

"How about the girl?"

The trooper who had covered her helped her to her feet. "Okay, I think."

For a long moment Ernest looked at Kay. "So I lost again." The resonance was gone from his face as he realized how much he had lost. "I just didn't get the breaks." He went unresistingly.

"What he valued most," Kay said, breaking a long silence, "was space and freedom and privacy. He'll never have them again, will he?"

"I sincerely hope not," Sylvia said. "When I got you undressed last night and saw your body — as though a tiger had clawed you, scratches on your sides and back and bleeding in half a dozen places — I regretted the passing of the electric chair."

As the telephone rang, Kay sat alert but dropped back in her chair when Charlie spoke to the editor of the village weekly, explaining that he'd give him the story the following day.

"Expecting a call?" Sylvia asked casually.

"Oh, no, nothing in particular."

"We've been keeping away callers," Charlie explained.

"After all the talking you had to do to the troopers this morning, we thought you'd had enough."

"Yes, I guess so."

"Now you have your money back I don't suppose you'll stay up here," Sylvia suggested.

"I don't know; I hadn't thought about it."

"That Treasury man left this morning. I don't

243

imagine there's anything to keep Deke Ransom now," Charlie commented. "When he had told us the whole story — about his brother and the things that had happened to you — Sylvia nearly hit the roof."

"One thing," Sylvia said, "chicken pox or no chicken pox, you're going to stay right here under our eyes."

"I never really understood how they found us," Kay said.

"Well, the manager at the motel picked up your address book and saw your name and the word 'Help!' scrawled in lipstick. He thought it was just a gag. Then a patrol car came by and told about the search for Kay Forbes, kidnaped by a man in a stolen Ford. The manager said the only Ford that had come in had 'Just Married' signs on it, but something clicked and he remembered the name in your address book.

"So they were waiting at the door when the waiter came from the restaurant. The manager was pleased as punch because he'd got Ernest right in the eye. Said he'd played ball as a kid."

Sylvia added abruptly, "It's all over, Kay. Stop looking so — defeated. This is victory, girl."

"I've got to get on a witness stand and send him to prison for the rest of his life," Kay said.

Charlie grunted. "Ask Mrs. Dan Ransom how she feels. If there's one thing I have no patience with it is sentimentality. If you are going to feel guilty about Ernest, don't tell us."

"It's always smart to listen to Charlie," Sylvia

said. "You give her some sound advice, my love."

"The oracle has already spoken," Charlie said smugly. "I told this wench to marry Ransom and take him out of circulation."

"There's only one objection that I can see," Kay said.

"What's that?"

"He hasn't asked me."

"Oh, if that's all —"

"Suppose," Deke began as he came into the room, "you let me speak for myself."

Charlie dragged Sylvia toward the door. He turned back. "If you can't talk him into it," he told Kay, "just call for me. I keep a shotgun for occasions like this."

When he had closed the living room door, he said, "Hey, I wonder if Ransom has had chicken pox. I'd better —"

He opened the door, stood staring, his round face beaming. Then he closed the door quietly.

"Well?" Sylvia demanded.

"Very."

DATE DUE		
MAY 1 6 1998		
Renew JUNES		
JUL 2 3 1998		
SF SEP 1999		
EE DEC 1999		
SJ FEB 2000		
DEC 0 9 2000		
JAN 0 7 2004		
FEB 2 8 2006		

DATE DUE		
JUN 1 4 2007		
SC OCT 2007		
AT JUL 2008		